GLITTER IN THE STARS

SPACE JANITOR THREE

JULIA HUNI

IPH MEDIA

Cover designed by German Creative

Julia Huni
Visit my website at juliahuni.com

IPH Media

BOOKS BY JULIA HUNI

Colonial Explorer Corps Series:

The Earth Concurrence

The Grissom Contention

The Saha Declination

Colonial Explorer Corps (books 1-3)

Recycled World Series:

Recycled World

Reduced World

Space Janitor Series:

The Vacuum of Space

The Dust of Kaku

The Trouble with Tinsel

Orbital Operations

Glitter in the Stars

Sweeping S'Ride

Triana Moore, Space Janitor (the complete series)

Tales of a Former Space Janitor

The Rings of Grissom

Planetary Spin Cycle

Waxing the Moon of Lewei

The Phoenix and Katie Li

Luna City Limited

Krimson Empire (with Craig Martelle):

Krimson Run

Krimson Spark

Krimson Surge

Krimson Flare

Krimson Empire (the complete series)

If you enjoy this story, sign up for my newsletter, at juliahuni.com and you'll get free prequels and short stories, plus get notifications when the next book is ready.

For my father-in-law, Robert
One of my favorite readers

CHAPTER ONE

CROSSING the cargo bay requires timing, speed, and an unhealthy disregard for human life. Your own life, that is. If you get crushed by a cargo bot, you better hope it kills you. Because if it doesn't, you'll spend the rest of your life paying off the damage assessment.

I've been prowling around the cargo bays for years without getting hurt. Although, to be honest, it doesn't really require anything except a good eye for patterns. Or access to the cargo bay schedules, so you can look for down times.

My name is Triana Moore, and I'm a station maintenance technician, so I have access to virtually everything on the station. I'm also the daughter of the chair of the station board of directors, which grants its own gold-card access. I try not to use that unless I absolutely have to—explaining to my mother would be worse than paying off the damage assessment.

Tonight, Charlie Bay is quiet. Bots are unloading a freighter from Grissom over in Bravo Bay, and there's a cruise liner taking on supplies at Delta. But the last ship docked at Charlie left two hours ago, and the next one isn't due until morning.

With a wave of my holo-ring, the door to Charlie's control booth slides open and lights spring on. I take a quick look at the console, but all readings are nominal. Out in the bay, five neatly arranged stacks of crates wait for tomorrow's ship. I squint at the markings—looks like Kakuvian brandy from the surface and a shipment of zero-grav veggies from the farm levels. The brandy might merit some extra security scans, but it won't require eyes-on inspection until just before loading.

I dim the windows so lights from the bay won't disturb me. Then I hook my hammock into the tie down rings—thoughtfully placed at chest height so workers can tether in the event of gravity loss—and climb in for the night.

THUMP.

My eyes pop open and I stare into the darkness. The glow from the console power button gives the ceiling a faint blue tinge. I peek over the edge of the hammock, but the console itself is dark.

I lay back and listen. The faint, ever present hiss of the air handlers sounds loud when I'm paying attention, but that's all I hear. Wait. What is that? A kind of sliding sound, like something heavy being dragged across carpet.

I lean out of the hammock and reach for the window control. The hammock swings and I grab at the console edge to steady myself. My fingers smack the edge of the console, but I can't—-waaaaghh!

Lying on the floor, I stare up at the dimly lit ceiling. From down here, I feel a rumbling vibration and shuddering thud. Something is going on in the cargo bay.

Rubbing my backside, I climb to my feet and clear the windows. The cargo bay looks just like it did last night. Six neat stacks of crates, waiting for the—

Hang on. Weren't there five stacks last night?

The sixth stack doesn't really merit the name. It's two small crates, about a meter square and maybe two meters long. They have no visible markings, so I fire up the console to consult the manifest. Probably just a late delivery, but I'm awake now, and curious.

Tomorrow's ship is a freighter headed for Sarvo Six. That's out on the fringes and we're the last stop before the long transit. The manifest still shows a huge shipment of Kakuvian brandy and a small produce pickup. Probably to be consumed by the crew on the way—the produce, not the brandy. Although the total bottle count might decrease by the time they arrive. Fresh fruits and veggies are provided by most big freighters to keep crew from jumping to another ship, and a tiny discrepancy in the brandy count will probably be overlooked. Good crew are hard to keep these days.

That's odd. No other items appear on the manifest. It's possible they were misrouted. I snoop around through the data for a few minutes, but no one has flagged a missing shipment, yet.

I look out the window again. There is something odd about those two crates. Beads of moisture have gathered along the sides of the crates. They almost appear to be... sweating? With a shrug, I crank up the lights and head out into the cargo bay.

A rapidly drying trail of splotches leads from the internal station doors, across the wide bay to the crates. Whatever it is, it's leaking, which is not good. I follow the trail to the crates, and walk around them, shining a focused beam from my holo onto the shadowed side of the boxes. No markings, anywhere. No shipping chip, no bar codes.

A bead of moisture collects on the corner of the top crate. It grows, clinging to the edge, then lets go, sliding down the side. Eyes narrowing, I reach out towards the rolling drip. This crate isn't leaking. It's melting.

I yank my hand back before touching the crate and spin on my heels. I run back to the control booth. It takes three tries before I manage to get my hammock down and bundled back into its conveniently attached packing bag. I take a swift look around to make sure I've left no evidence and scoot out the door.

The warehouse takes up most of Levels 36 and 37. The ring of cargo bays occupies the outer ring, but the rest is a massive open space with bots pushing cargo from one bay to another and into the huge cargo float to distribute items to the rest of the station. I find a convenient stack of crates and sit down, flicking my holo-ring. A quick hack erases my visit to the cargo bay. Then I call Station Operations.

"Ops, Carter." A small bald man with bright green eyes and a neck tattoo answers the call.

"Carter, it's Moore," I say. "I'm off duty, but I need to report a cargo issue."

"Triana, it's oh-dark-thirty!" He peers around me, obviously reading the data on his screen. "What are you doing in Cargo if you're off duty?"

I shrug. "Couldn't sleep, figured a walk would help."

"A walk—through Cargo?" He gives me a look. "Does Kara have a visitor again? You can always crash in my place."

"Thanks, Carter, but I'm fine. Besides I don't think your partner would appreciate me randomly barging in."

Carter waves his bony hand. "Not a problem. We've all had roommates before. Tracy gets it. But that's not why you called."

I flick a picture of the drip trail to him. "I noticed something dripping. I followed the trail to Charlie, but it's dried up now. You might want to send someone in to investigate."

A smile flashes across Carter's narrow face. "You must be tired. You forgot to strip the metadata, Triana. It places you *inside* Charlie."

Zark.

He laughs. "Don't worry, I deleted it. I'll send Farquad up on a 'routine' check. You mind waiting to show him what's going on?"

"I don't think he'll need me to show him," I say. "But I'll wait."

I look for a place to stash my bag but give up after a few minutes. Carter obviously knows why I'm here, and I'm sure Farq does, too. He's the biggest gossip in the station. I dash across the warehouse to wait for him by the float tubes in the center of the huge space. Forget what I said about crossing a cargo bay—if you want to take your life in your hands, try crossing the warehouse at peak time. It's like playing that Ancient Earth vid game with the frog.

A few minutes later, Farq steps out of the float tube. I'm pretty tall for a woman, but Farq makes me feel tiny. He's well over two meters tall—tall enough he has to duck to go through a standard sized door—and broad as a planet. His dark skin contrasts beautifully with his white teeth and sparkling gray eyes. Blond dreadlocks fall to the middle of his back, but since he's on duty, they're tied neatly back into a bundle.

"Yo, Tree, talk to me!" He smiles and slaps me on the shoulder. I stumble and catch my balance against a nearby crate. "I hear you discovered a mysterious trail of moisture!" His voice, like the rest of him, is huge.

He leads the way down the brightly marked safety path, carefully staying between the lines and stopping at the crossings. Farq rolls his eyes at me. I shrug and we both laugh. No doubt this "routine" check is being recorded, or Farq would have bounded across the space like I did earlier. Safety first, at least when the boss is watching.

Farq opens Charlie Bay and we hike across the empty space to the six stacks of crates. I half expected the mystery boxes to be gone, but they're sitting there, dripping like crazy. In fact, a puddle has formed around the bottom one. We exchange looks, and Farq calls Ops.

"You seein' this, Carter?" He asks, ignoring the standard protocol. "There's no ID and it looks like the box piddled on the rug." He waves a device near the box and puddle. "Nothing on the haz scan, so I'm going to open her up."

"Roger," Carter replies, his formality a rebuke. "Proceed with extraction."

I snicker and Farq grins.

"Proceeding as ordered," he replies in a robotic voice, shaking his head. He hooks his scanner onto his belt and pulls out another device. He reaches up and attaches it to the top corner of the upper crate. The device latches onto the corner and begins cutting around the top edge like an Ancient Earth can opener.

If I stand on my tippy toes, I can peek over the top edge, but I can't really see inside. "Can you see anything up there?" Farq's extra centimeters give him a distinct advantage.

"Nothin' to see. Grab a lifter, will you?"

While the cutter whirs away, I trot across the bay and pull one of the box lifters from the rack by its convenient handle. Bots do most of the heavy lifting, but these hand-held anti-grav lifters make shifting cargo much easier in tight spaces. I grab a second lifter and head back to Farq.

When the cutter finishes its circuit, Farq unclips it and sticks it back into his belt pouch. The smell of hot plastek curls the hairs inside my nose. He attaches a lifter to one end of the box lid and turns it on. With a soft hum the lifter lights up. Farq presses the link sequencer to connect the two lifters and attaches the second one to the other end. He presses a green lighted button. The lifters whine and with a grate and a chunk, the lid comes loose. He tugs the closest handle towards us, and the whole lid slides forward.

"Saints and angels preserve us!" Farq stares down into the box, transfixed. His hand makes a ritual gesture, seemingly without input from his brain.

"What?" I cry, jumping up and down like a spoiled child. "I can't see! What is it?"

"Not what," Farq says, still staring into the crate. "Who."

CHAPTER TWO

I SLUMP against a crate in the warehouse, exhausted. I've repeated my discovery story three times already for the different levels of station security. I'm sticking with the story I told Carter about noticing the drips outside, and he and Farq have backed me up. I hope Carter really did delete that picture. If I had more energy, I'd hack into his account and make sure.

Sliding down onto the crate, I lean my head against the bulkhead and close my eyes. The noise around me becomes a soothing drone, and I start to drift off. The Supreme Emperor of the Bots, who looks strangely like Hy-Mi in a silver suit, offers me a medal for superior loop hacking. "I'd rather have a Slami-n-Chēz," I mutter.

"I have some chocolate. Will that do?" Ty O'Neill stands before me, shiny and perfect as ever, with a gold embossed box in his hand.

I check the time. "How do you look so put-together at four in the morning? And do you always carry candy with you?" I take the box and open the lid, breathing in the unmistakable scent of Dolce Amour Chocolates.

"Bodies in the cargo hold in the dark of night shift? That has Triana Moore written all over it." He grins, dodging my half-hearted slap. "I reviewed the unboxing vid while I got dressed, so I knew you'd be here. My question is: *why* were you here?"

"Can't talk. Eating chocolate," I mumble.

"I'll be back. Don't go anywhere." He gently yanks one of my frizzy red curls. I give him a thumbs up and settle back against the crate, the chocolate cradled lovingly in my lap.

I watch O'Neill stride away towards Charlie Bay. He really is about perfect. Wavy brown hair, chocolate eyes, and an excellent butt. His pants are tight enough to show it off, but loose enough to leave something to the imagination. I've spent more time than I care to discuss thinking about his pants. Okay, that really didn't come out the way I meant it, so I'm going to focus on this chocolate.

Half-way through the third piece, a pair of Emergency Med Techs rolls a med-pod out of the bay and across to the cargo tube. Another pair follows close behind with a second one. O'Neill jogs across the warehouse to talk to the EMTs then returns to me.

"Those were med-pods." I lick the chocolate from my fingers. "Did someone get hurt?"

O'Neill stares at me for a beat. "No. Those were for the two people in the crates. They're alive."

"What? Where did they come from? Why were they in there?"

He shakes his head. "We don't have any answers—they're both unconscious. But I'll interview them as soon as they wake up." He picks up my bag. "You don't need to stay here any longer. They got your statements. I'll walk you home."

"No, I'm not going home. Erco is visiting, and I promised Kara she could have the place to herself. That's why I was here."

"You were sleeping in the cargo bay? Why didn't you go up to 83?"

I just look at him. "Not going to happen."

"I thought you and your mother worked out some kind of truce." He puts his warm hand on my back and ushers me towards the float tubes.

"Yeah, she stays out of my life, and I stay out of hers."

"Ok, look, why don't you stay at my place?" I start to protest but he cuts me off. "I have to go to the office to deal with all this, so you'll have it to yourself. Go get some sleep." He flicks an unlock code to my ring and kisses my cheek. Then he steps into the up tube and zips away.

With a mental shrug, I take the down tube to Level 27. I'm too tired to think about anything right now, and there's no way I can camp out in cargo with all this going on. I stumble out of the float tube, down Radial 10 and out to A Ring. Ty's door slides open when I approach, in response to the unlock code. I drop my bag next to the couch, dim the windows, and fall onto the bed. In seconds, I'm out.

At eight fifteen, my holo-ring wakes me with a message requesting my presence in the penthouse suite.

CHAPTER THREE

AS I OPEN THE DOOR, the sweet, buttery, caramel smell of freshly baked chocolate chip cookies wafts out into the lobby. My stomach grumbles, and my steps quicken as I move into the foyer. The door shuts behind me with a soft thud and snick. I follow my nose through the living room and into the study.

Dav, my mother's chef and pastry expert, smiles at me. He sets a green-trimmed china plate and a crystal goblet of milk on a side table by a plush Lether chair.

"Are those for me?" I ask.

"Of course, Sera Morgan. Your mother doesn't eat cookies."

"That's always made me a bit suspicious of her. And don't call me Sera Morgan. I go by Triana, now." I reach for the plate, but my hand stops halfway there. "Did she tell you to bake these?"

Dav shakes his head. "At ten o'clock in the morning? No. She told me you'd be coming up. I knew you'd want a snack, so I made your favorite. They are still your favorite, I hope?"

"Oh, yeah." I take a bite and nearly groan in ecstasy. "I don't know what your secret is Dav, but I've tried every chocolate chip cookie in the Auto-Kich'n molecular maps, none of them taste like this!"

Dav smiles again. "I've been very careful to make sure my cookies never leave this compartment. You're the only one allowed to take them out, and that's only because I know you'd never sell me out. But even if AutoMap Labs got ahold of one, they can't replicate it. The molecular maps are too homogenous. Food made by human hands is never that perfect, and that's what makes it perfect."

"Wow," I mumble through another mouthful, "that's pretty deep."

He shrugs. "It's my passion. Come by the kitchen before you leave and I'll pack up a bag for you." With another smile, he heads out of the room.

The next five minutes are warm, sweet, crunchy-yet-chewy, chocolate bliss.

Until she walks in. "Good morning, Annabelle." My mother smooths down her blue silk suit and sinks gracefully to the extreme edge of the massive chair behind the even more massive desk. "Thank you for joining me. I need to ask you for a favor."

"Good to see you, too, Mother. What can I do for you?" I set the last cookie back onto the plate, untasted. I knew they were to butter me up. That's why she told Dav I was coming—because she knew he'd make cookies.

"The Major Family meeting is on Sally Ride next month. I will attend virtually, of course, but I can't attend in person. As you know, each Family sends a representative to the meeting each standard year. I would like you to represent the Family."

My jaw drops. "You want me to represent the Morgans? But I don't want to!" My brain has frozen—I can't come up with a decent argument. "I resigned as the Morgan heir! That's why I ran away! Why I changed my name! What do you not understand about that?"

"Annabelle, I've allowed you this temporary 'escape' for the last six years." Her voice takes on a hard edge. As she speaks, Dav returns with a tray of tea, and Mother nods her thanks. She picks up the china cup and saucer. "It's time for you to return to the family and take up your responsibilities."

I grind my teeth. This is exactly why I ran away. I decide to try to be reasonable. "Mother, I can't go to S'Ride. I have a job, and I only have three days of vacation time."

She waves her hand. "Hy-Mi will deal with that."

"NO!" I leap out of my chair. Hy-Mi is her personal assistant, and everyone on the station knows who he works for. "They don't know I'm Annabelle Morgan, and I don't want them to know! Please, Mother, send someone else. The Families will accept Hy-Mi as your rep. They all know him. And really, the idea that someone has to attend in person is archaic."

"Archaic or not, someone must go." She fixes her icy blue eyes on me. "And it is time that you step up and prove yourself."

I open and close my mouth a couple times, pacing around the room. Arguments pop into my brain and get shunted back out just as quickly. None of them will satisfy the all-controlling Ice Dame. And she holds all the cards. With one word, she could get me fired and thrust back into the life I left behind six years ago.

I turn towards her. "Look. Let me see what I can work out. I really don't want to do this, but I understand you need my help. Please, don't blow my cover! I can't stay in the MCC if they know who I am, and I love that job. Give me a few days to come up with something."

Mother picks up her cup again, her lips curved infinitesimally. I hate that smug smile. "Done. I'll give you three days. Then Hy-Mi will make arrangements."

"Fine!" I storm out the door. At the threshold, I pause.

"Did you need something, Annabelle?" Mother says to my back.

I turn and stomp back into the room. "Just my cookie." I grab the last one and run.

KARA STEPS BACK against the closed door of our new compartment on Level 6 and gazes around the empty room. "This is spectacular!"

"That might be a bit of an overstatement," I reply. "But it's definitely an improvement over the studio." I stand in the middle of the empty space, gazing up at the huge holo-window. The view is as beautiful as O'Neill's up on Level 27. The sun, out of sight to the left, glints off one of the oceans on Kaku.

This compartment also has a bedroom, which will make my life much easier when Kara has a visitor. It will cost us more and moving all our stuff will be a pain. We've been on the waiting list for a larger space for weeks, but the housing market is pretty tight on the station. In fact, I thought it would be months before we'd find a place we can afford. When Kara got the call this morning, we were both shocked.

"Did Erco bribe someone to bump us up the list?" I ask. "You two seem to be getting pretty serious."

Kara blushes but ignores my comment. "I thought maybe your mother had helped out with the rental waitlist."

I slide down the wall to sit on the floor. "I don't think Mother had anything to do with this. I certainly didn't mention it."

Kara plops down beside me. "Have you figured out what to do about the S'Ride thing?" She pulls a packet of chips out of her bag, pops it open, and offers it to me.

I take a handful and shake my head. "Ugh, don't remind me. If I don't come up with something by tomorrow, I'm toast. I may as well move back into *her* place."

"If that deal didn't include the Ice Dame herself, I'd ask you to take me with you." Kara does a dramatic shudder then pats my arm. "Don't worry, you'll come up with something. You always do."

"Yeah, but it might involve running away again," I mutter. My ring pings, so I lick the salt off my fingers and check my messages. "Perfect, a message from Rash." Kendrick al-Rashid-Thompson is the Operations Supervisor and basically my boss. He oversees all the humans who keep Station Kelly-Kornienko—commonly known as "SK2"—working. I flick the message open and hear his voice in my ear.

"Moore, you've been temporarily reassigned. Check in with me before your shift tomorrow for details. Al-Rashid-Thompson out."

I let my head thunk against the wall. "Reassigned? Again? I just got off my suspension! That class was supposed to get me out of the dog house and back onto the regular rotation." I had been suspended for a—let's call it a "miscommunication." I completed a refresher course down on Kaku weeks ago and was reinstated. But thanks to the way scheduling is done, I'm still working in the repair station. "Or maybe he means I've been reassigned to the MCC where I belong?" I look hopefully to Kara.

She shrugs. "Ya got me. Why don't you ask him?"

I check the status board. "He must have scheduled that message to go out just as his shift ended, the little rat! He's off duty as of three minutes ago. I'll have to wait until morning. He'll skewer me if I call him while he's off duty."

Kara pushes up off the floor. "Let's start moving, then. That will take your mind off it, and make you tired enough to sleep all night."

CHAPTER FOUR

AFTER A LONG EVENING of carting stuff up the cargo tube—working in station maintenance has some perks—I slept pretty well. This morning, I arrive at Operations thirty minutes before my assigned shift. Since I'm slated to work in Repair, I'll need a little extra time to get down to the lower levels. Float tube traffic is pretty heavy at oh-eight-hundred on the station.

Farq gives me a little wave from behind his console as I stride into the Ops Center. Carter, the night shift supervisor, glances up as I approach the central station and jerks his head towards the break room. I give him a little nod and angle across the crowded center, dodging drowsy controllers in wheeled office chairs. Most of them barely notice my passage, but a few look up and give me a fist bump.

The break room has seen better days. SK2 is one of the older stations, and the operational parts haven't received the same expensive makeovers as the upper levels. Wealthy stockholders never visit the control center, so we make do with the coffee-stained tables, threadbare carpet, and scuffed furniture.

I check out the donuts in a box on the table. One has a hole poked in it, and the glaze has melted off the other two and slid down into a puddle gluing them to the bottom of the box. Never mind.

"Thanks for coming in early, Moore." Rash leans against the worn counter, his ancient coffee mug cradled in one hand. The other hand rapidly flicks through a social media feed on his holo-ring.

"Hey boss, what's going on?" Although we always refer to him as "Rash," the entire ops team has learned not to use that name to his face. Whenever a newbie shows up, we hold a pool on when he'll do the deed. Never takes more than five days, and it never happens again after the first time.

Rash flicks open a document on his holo-ring. "I have an unusual assignment for you." He gives me a quizzical look.

"What?" I drop into a dingy chair and poke at the donuts with a plastek knife.

"I've never had a request like this come in before." He shakes his head. "They asked for a maintenance tech with top notch programming skills, and basic experience in physiotherapy nano-bot programming, station comms, networking, med pod troubleshooting, and cargo bot repair. It's almost as if they wrote the request with you in mind."

I stare at him. Before I found my current job in maintenance, I kind of bounced around the station, doing a few weeks' work here and there, trying to find the right fit. That list could have been pulled directly from my records. It has Hy-Mi written all over it. "What's the assignment?"

He tosses a requisition code to my holo-ring. "Cruise ship. CSS Morningstar. Owned by Pleiades StarCruises which is a subsidiary of MBP Industries. MBP also owns SK'Corp, of course. One of their maint techs quit over on Grissom, and they've been running short-handed. Second one got a job offer down on Kaku and will be leaving the ship when they dock here. Company doesn't have anyone available locally, so they asked if we could loan them a tech with that set of skills. Luckily for them, you aren't on the regular rotation yet. Do you want it?"

"Let me guess." I flick the document open. "They need me for the run from here to Sally Ride."

Rash tilts his head, narrowing his eyes. "How did you know that?"

I shrug, scrolling through the requisition. "That's the standard run for most cruisers, right? Grissom, Kaku, S'Ride." I have to admire Hy-Mi's resourcefulness. How many strings did he have to pull to get a job offer dirtside for the ship's maint tech? That can't have been cheap. I wave my hand through the accept icon and flip the virtual document back to him.

"They're going to send me back on the company dime. Kind of a mandatory vacation. Can't complain about that. You'll have me on the regular rotation when I return, right?"

"Yeah, I'll take care of it. I don't want to lose you." He swipes his hand through the document, approving it, and sends it into the ether.

"Wow, boss, don't get all weepy-eyed on me. I'll be back."

"I'm not worried about that. You always turn up. Now get down to Repair and let me get to work."

WHEN O'NEILL STOPS by the repair shop around noon, I'm ready to take a break. I put my tools away and wave my holo-ring through the clock-out icon by the door. We tromp out to the float tube up to my favorite deli on Level 9.

"So, what's going on with those frozen people?" I step into the line outside the deli. The concourse is crowded with noisy, harried lower-Levs on their lunch hour. The smell of fried foods, spicy condiments, and preservative-laden meats wraps around me in a comforting blanket.

O'Neill doesn't look as content. He casts a doubtful look at the tray full of tempura veggies being carried past. His eyes range over the crowd but settle back on me with an almost audible snap. He shrugs. "We're not really sure. Andrus Mohammed is from Grissom. Patrina del Fragoso is from New Deseret. They both have memory gaps ranging back about six months. The last thing they remember is their normal lives at home. We don't know how they got to SK2 or even when they got here. There's no identifying information on the crates. There's no obvious connection between them. We're trying to track them backwards, but there are significant gaps in the OS tracking data. Including a strange two-minute gap in the vid from Charlie Bay." He raises an eyebrow at me.

I grimace. "That might have been me. I was in the Charlie Bay control room when the crates showed up. I went out to look at them, but I didn't want the official report to show that I had been there, so I edited the data before calling it in."

O'Neill heaves a sigh. "You know you make my life a lot harder?"

"But I'm worth it, right?" I grin hopefully. The woman in front of me moves away from the window, and I step up to order my favorite sandwich and fries. As usual, O'Neill gets a milkshake and carrots with his sub. "Carrots? Again? You aren't fooling anyone with that Ser Healthy business. And you can just keep your mitts off my fries."

We take our food to a window seat in the green space on Level 10. We're on the dark side of the station right now, and the stars spread out before us in a twinkling blanket. I glance up at the port arms jutting out from Level 40. Three arms on this side are empty, but a new ship berthed this morning, and the scan bots scurry around, checking for structural weaknesses. A hold breach in deep space is nasty.

"I'm sure you've heard I'll be shipping out tomorrow morning." I pull a fry off my tray.

O'Neill's lips quirk. "I probably knew that before you did."

"What do you mean?" I pick up my sandwich.

"Hy-Mi asked for help getting you on board with the plan. He suggested I invite you to join me for a romantic get-away." He gives me a sideways glance.

My mouth falls open. "Wow. I hope you told him to suck vacuum."

"I wasn't quite that expressive," he says. "I did tell him that our personal lives were none of his business, and I wouldn't allow him to use me as a pawn. Then I suggested he find you a job."

"I was wondering how that happened. It seemed too subtle for Mother's normal interference. I mean, Hy-Mi is great at that kind of stuff, but Mother was planning on just yanking me out of the MCC and telling them to deal with it."

"He was headed that direction. I just gave him a gentle push." He takes one of my fries, and I pretend not to notice. "Are you packed?"

I laugh. "According to the ship stats, I have room for three uniforms, which will be issued on board, and assigned storage for a single set of 'off-duty clothing' which can only be worn dirtside. Hy-Mi messaged me thirty minutes ago that he's already shipped the appropriate apparel for my appearance at the Family Meeting. I don't think packing will take long."

He reaches for a second fry, and this time I fix a steely glare on him. His hand moves closer to the fries, and I narrow my eyes. He gives me the puppy dog face. I relent. I shouldn't eat them, anyway. I already sent my measurements to the ship for uniforms. "You don't seem very unhappy that I'm leaving for two weeks."

He dips a handful of fries into the sauce. "Didn't I tell you? I'm going, too."

CHAPTER FIVE

I SHOULD HAVE REALIZED Mother wouldn't send me without a Board Security agent. "Really? You aren't interested in taking me on a romantic get-away, but you'll go along as security? I guess the per diem must be attractive." I give him the stink eye.

He holds up his hands to ward me off. "I'd be happy to take you on a romantic get-away. I just didn't want to be manipulated into it by Hy-Mi."

"Yeah, I know. What's your cover?" I grab the last two fries before he can scarf them.

"No cover. The Board is sending me to liaise with the security manager at the Family Meeting on Sally Ride." He leans back and sips his milkshake.

"Are you kidding me? You get to lounge around as a passenger, and I have to work all the way there?"

"You could have travelled in comfort as Annabelle Morgan. But you insisted on maintaining your current identity and job. And it's not my fault you don't have any vacation time." He stacks our trays and stands.

"What about you? How much vacation do you have?" I scramble out of my seat and follow him to the door.

"It doesn't matter, because this is a business trip for me." He smiles.

Grr.

THE NEXT MORNING, I arrive at the cargo bay at five. The crew loading areas are long, narrow, gray rooms located between the cargo bays. The CSS Morningstar docked at Delta bay last night. Passengers had the evening and all of today to explore the station, take a lightning fast excursion to the surface, or just lounge around the ship. Relief crew, like me, report this morning, to allow current crew members a few hours of "shore" leave.

A gaggle of teens huddles at the near end of the room. I stroll over, feeling older and wiser, even though I'm barely twenty-four standard years. "Hi, I'm Triana. Maintenance technician. What will you all be doing?"

They stare at me, at each other, at the floor. I smile encouragingly, and they all start to babble at once. Finally, a dark-haired girl overrides the others, and their voices peter out.

"I'm Ambar. We're, all of us—" She waves around at the group, as if I couldn't figure out who she meant. "—hospitality students from the Techno-Inst down on Kaku. This is our first-year field training. We do a leg as stewards, then we'll take a turn at dining staff, and whoever does the best gets to do the last stint as junior purser. The rest have to do kitchen help. That's Sandrine, Zibia, Arstend, Tei Chaia, and Steve." She points to each of her friends as she recites the names, but it's too quick for me to put them together.

I spread a general smile around the group. "Who decides who's best?"

Ambar raises her chin, as if challenging her classmates to even attempt to beat her. "We wear body cams when we're on duty." She taps her name badge. A green bullseye sticker—required by Kaku law for all surveillance devices—covers half her name. "We have to pull the stickers off when we board. The instructors watch all our work, observe our interactions with the passengers and other crew. They also give us duty challenges. Those are specially engineered situations to test our customer service abilities. Each evening, they review all our interactions and activities from the previous twenty-four hours. Then they rank us for the next day. If you do really well in the rankings, you start out the next day with extra points. The worst performer each day starts out with a deficit. Whoever gets the most points by the time we reach Sally Ride, gets the junior purser slot."

I blink. I've seen something like this on *Ancient TēVē*. They called it a "reality show." I don't know where the name originates, as most of the shows had no connection to reality. At least, I don't think reality was that messed up on Ancient Earth, but who knows for sure?

A gong rings through the room, followed by loud and productive throat clearing. "Attention new hires. You are cleared to board. Follow your holo-rings through the airlock to Conference Room B. Repeat: Proceed through the airlock to Conference Room B." Loud static follows the announcement then cuts off abruptly. A door at the far end of the room pops open.

"I guess that's us then," I say cheerfully, shouldering my small bag. The students scramble around, repacking all the junk they had somehow spread around the gray room. I wait a minute, but they don't seem to make any progress. With a shrug, I step over and around them and through the door. A worn gray carpet leads up a ramp to the external wall, then into an airlock. I look behind me, but the kids aren't even moving yet. With a roll of my eyes, I slap the cycle button, and wait while the airlock does its thing.

About thirty seconds later, the other door pops open, and I step out onto the transfer tube platform. The airlock clanks shut behind me, and the tube gravitronics kick in. I whoosh up the steep tube to the platform outside the ship. I step onto the platform, and a flashing access panel tells me where to place my hand. The ship's operating system confirms my identity. Another set of airlocks lets me into the ship itself, and I follow my vibrating holo-ring down a short hall to Conference Room B.

I pause in the doorway. The room is painted a pale peach color, with a palm-wide, horizontal, teal stripe about a meter above the deck. Carpet with wave patterns in shades of maroon, garnet and puce covers the floor, but it is completely overwhelmed by a lime green conference table and twelve swivel chairs. I pull out the closest chair and drop into it, closing my eyes against the colorful assault.

"Just what the *broccoli* are you trying to pull?" Ambar growls, slamming one of her three bags against my shins. A confused look crosses her face. "What the *chowder*?"

I try to hide the smile tugging at my mouth. "The ship has profanity sensors. It replaces cursing with random words. They must have it set to food, today." I flick my holo-ring and pull up the ship's employment contract. "Here it is. The standard contract, which covers interns, gives them permission to add the SwearStop app remotely to your holo-ring. If it predicts profanity, it broadcasts a word in the right range and volume to suppress your voice. Didn't you read the contract before you swiped?"

"Seriously?" The boy with the black crew-cut asks. I think he is Tei Chaia. He lets out a string of words, at various tones. "*Nectarine, prosciutto, borscht! Liver, haggis*!" He gets louder with each word, until he shouts the last one. The matching OS broadcast, "*Crumpet!*" nearly deafens us. The busty blonde girl—Zibia?—winces and slaps him on the shoulder.

"That's so cool!" Tei Chaia grins.

"Whatever," Ambar says, her voice vicious. "I don't give a flying *anchovy* about the contract. What I care about is you trying to make the rest of us look bad."

I hold my hands up, palms out. "Cool your jets! I am not part of your crazy game. I graduated years ago and have a real job with a real company. I'm not in competition with any of you."

She narrows her eyes at me. "It's not a game, it's my future! And I don't care if you aren't part of the competition. Anything that makes me look bad is unacceptable. And I do not allow anyone to make me look bad. You've been warned." She swings around, slamming her bag into my legs again, and flounces to the other side of the table.

The rest of the kids take seats on either side of Ambar, staring across the table at me. I look at each of them in turn then scroll further down the contract that's still hovering over my palm. "I guess you also didn't notice that all on-duty conversations are recorded. And you went on duty when you authenticated your identity at the ship's airlock. According to section fourteen, subsection A, threatening other employees creates a hostile work environment and is considered harassment." I just made up that last part, but I'm betting Ambar doesn't know that.

"Actually, that's subsection G." A tall, thin woman walks in. She's dressed in the Pleiades StarCruises uniform of peach coverall with maroon piping and lime green epaulets. Three wide stripes on the epaulet, so she must be someone important. A liberal sprinkling of patches and buttons covers her chest. The lime green badge on her shoulder, with the word Morningstar in teal, identifies her as a member of this ship. Just looking at all those colors makes my eyes water. "You must be Technician Moore."

I stand up to bump fists with her. These military wanna-bees seem to like that kind of formality. She gives me the smallest of approving nods.

She turns to look at the teens on the far side of the table. "Since this is clearly your first adult employment opportunity, allow me to offer you some advice. Don't *tater-tot* with the maintenance crew. They can make your life miserable. Not that Technician Moore would do anything of the sort, I'm sure." She gives each of us a stern look.

"I am First Officer Malenda Frankl Ling Park Markowski al Tendi Jones. You may call me First Officer Frankl, or Ma'am. I do not answer to 'yo,' 'hey you,' or 'officer lady.' The captain, and *only* the captain, calls me 'Number One'.

"This may be a pleasure cruiser, but she is also a transport vessel. As such, she is run efficiently by her crew. We expect our crew, including our interns, to be professional, well-trained, team players. We also understand this is your first cruise. If you don't know how to do something, ask. If you don't know where something is, ask. The first time. If you need to ask a second time, you'd better start doing your homework." She gives each of us another hard look, then flicks her holo-ring.

"Interns, Assistant Purser Watkins will give you a tour and get you settled in your bunks and your new positions. Technician Moore, Maintenance Supervisor Santiago would like you to report to Operations immediately. She'll make sure you get oriented." As she steps back toward the door, a lanky young woman with two stripes on her epaulets walks in. She strides to the front of the room and the SmartWall behind her lights up with the words "Welcome, Interns."

"Thank you, Ma'am," she says to Frankl, with a salute. The first officer returns the salute and gestures to me to follow her out the door.

"Intern onboarding takes most of the day." As the door closes, she jerks her head at me and leads the way down the hall. "I've seen your record, so I know you've done all the standard MBP corporate training. Santiago will fill you in on anything we do differently here on the Morningstar. A smart diagram of the ship and the crew guide slips have been sent to your holo-ring. Take a second to approve the download, and then follow the priority slip to MCC. Welcome aboard." Without waiting for a reply, she whisks through a door marked Admin, leaving me alone in the hall.

CHAPTER SIX

I DOWNLOAD the files and follow the tug on my finger down the hallway. The ship is fifteen levels, from top to bottom, or whatever the nautical term is. Top and bottom don't really mean that much on a spaceship—it's not like the bottom is underwater. The lower levels are cargo and crew spaces, while the upper levels contain passenger accommodations and entertainment.

My ring takes me almost the full length of the ship, stopping at a door just ahead of the engine bulkhead. The unmarked hatch slides open when I reach it, and I step into a familiar looking room. It's laid out much like our Ops Center on the station, although this one is smaller. Three of the five workstations are empty.

A tiny, dark-haired woman looks up as I enter and waives me over. "I'm Lesli-Noor Santiago, Ops Supervisor. Call me Les. We're pretty informal down here in the bowels of the ship. As you know, we're down several crew members, so I'm not going to waste time on chit-chat. That's Ollie. Oliver Chattrakulrak." She jerks a thumb at the other occupant of the room.

Ollie, a bulky, bald man with dark skin and a full beard, waves and turns back to his screens.

Les gestures to the empty workstation next to Ollie. "Go ahead and log in there. I know you're used to having a separate MCC, but here on the ship we all work from Ops. Ollie will give you a hand if you get stuck on anything."

"Oh, okay." I thought I'd have time to get settled into my room. "I don't have any uniforms, yet." I drop my bag next to the console and sit down.

"They'll be delivered to your room," Les says. "You aren't going anywhere, today, and we don't care what you're wearing. If we need to send anyone to the passenger areas, Ollie or I can do it for now. Once we're underway, you'll have a chance to find your berth and get changed. Your login credentials are on your holo-ring with the rest of the files."

She turns back to her own screens, so I flick my holo-ring and pull up the files. I log in to the ship's system and a flood of reports streams up my screen. "Holy cow!"

"Do the red ones first," Ollie says, without looking away from his own data stream. About a third of the reports sport a red headline and flashing emergency icon. Thanks Ollie, I would never have thought of that.

Hours later, my stomach growls so loud I think the passengers must have heard it. Ollie, a man of few words, flicks me a colorful icon shaped like a sandwich.

The icon links to a menu with several items already selected. I click on a small pizza and a side salad then flick the "send order" button. The menu folds up like origami into an arrow which sails away into nothingness. A countdown timer appears on my screen under the words "Scheduled Delivery" flashing in matching green script.

I stand up and stretch my neck, shoulders, and arms. Then I walk around the small room, trying to get my blood flowing again. In the MCC on station, I don't have a lot of space, but the setup requires me to move around the room. I glance at Ollie, but he hasn't stirred since I arrived. His chair reclines so far, his back is parallel to the floor, and the screens are arranged above and around him in a hemisphere of data.

"How'd you change the angle of your chair like that?" I ask. It doesn't look remotely comfortable, but if he can lean it back that much, surely there's a way to raise mine.

Ollie grunts and flicks another icon at me. This one is a shortcut to the workstation manual, with the chair and desk adjustments flagged.

"I guess you get asked that a lot?"

Ollie gives me a thumbs up without even looking my way.

I flip through the manual, then play with the angle and height of my workstation. I'm still not happy with the adjustment when the countdown hits zero and the door chimes. I swivel around as it opens.

A small cube, about a half-meter on each side, glides into the room. It navigates around Les's central console and slides to a halt by Ollie. He flicks a couple icons, and his rig rotates until he's upright. The cube rises on a set of accordion arms, until it's desk height. A door pops open, and Ollie extracts his food. He pats the top of the box, and the door closes. The bot drops back to floor level and zips over to me.

I take my food, inhaling the scent of yeasty, toasty crust, melted cheese, and spicy sauce. A holo pops up over the bot, asking if I'd like to add a beverage to my order. I wave my hand through the 'yes' icon, and a door on the end pops open displaying a bev dispenser.

"I need one of these on the station." I take the frosty glass.

Ollie grunts and smiles over his massive sandwich. "That's why I work here."

At least, I think that's what he says. Between his low volume and mouthful of turkey, bacon, and 'cado, it's a little hard to decipher. I smile and turn back to my lunch.

I MAY NEVER WALK AGAIN.

Les finally returned to Ops, with a tall, thin woman following behind. "This is Kindra. She's the night shift Maintainer."

"Hi, I'm Triana." I try to slide gracefully out of my chair. My right leg is asleep, and my butt hurts. I push myself up with a groan. My foot buckles, and I stumble, grabbing the seat back to stop my fall.

Kindra laughs. "I remember my first shift! You gotta get up and move around! Turn on some music and shake your thing!" She flicks her holo-ring, and loud *techno-fierdi* starts pumping through the room. Kindra breaks into an impromptu dance routine. Stick-like arms and legs flail through the air, barely missing me. Her green and purple striped hair whips around her head in wild abandon.

Les swipes a hand through the air, and the music drops to a whisper. She smiles. "Supervisor override. You know I hate that stuff, Kin." Les tosses the woman a small object. "And get that hair under control."

Kindra rolls her eyes, but obediently gathers her hair into a neat bundle at her neck. "No one's gonna see me down here." She strides over to the chair on Ollie's far side and sheds her wrinkled jacket. She tosses it onto the chair, which she sends spinning away from the console. With a swift movement, she pops the desk up to standing height and flicks on the control screens.

"You still need to maintain the dress code, Kindra." Les sighs. "Besides, you never know when you might need to go upstairs."

"Can't let the passengers see me with my hair down," Kindra grouses. She scrolls through some screens. "Hey, Triana, you did a good job catching up on the backlog! Nice work." She gives me a smile and turns to her console, flicking open more holo-screens.

"Ollie, quitting time," Les says. "Random will be here any minute." She glares at the clock projected on the wall, as if she blames it for Random's tardiness.

Ollie flicks a few screens and starts the chair rotation sequence. When he reaches vertical, he pushes back, and slides out of the contraption. I blink at his hover chair—I hadn't even noticed it inside the station. His adaptive device whirs softly and raises him to standing height. His legs are missing below mid-thigh. That kind of disability can be easily remedied before a person reaches full growth, so his must have occurred after he reached adulthood. Still, a hoverchair is unusual for a young person. Most would opt for prosthetics, which are almost as good as natural legs. Sometimes better.

The door swishes open and a deep, rich voice echoes through Ops. "The king of swing, the baron of *bachata*, the *fincadi* of *fierdi* has arrived!" A short, dark man in impeccable uniform explodes into the room. His bright green eyes sparkle and his white teeth gleam. He makes a sharp gesture and the *techno-fierdi* blasts out again. Kindra starts a cha-cha at her desk. Random grabs her hand, swinging her through a fast series of spins and a dip. The music drops down to a murmur.

"I feel like I've been dropped into a musical." I limp across the small room and hold out a fist. "Triana Moore."

"Random Garcia Jones." He grins, bowing with a flourish, then bumping my fist. "Night ops and amateur dance instructor."

Les groans and rubs her hand over her face. "Are you on again, Random?"

Random holds up his hands, palms out. "Not this time. I've offered to do a little consulting, but I'm not a primary." He turns to me. "The Morningstar is famous for our dance competition: *Dancing in the Stars*. Each leg of the journey, members of the crew partner with passengers to learn a dance routine. The last night in transit, we hold the competition. I've won five of the last seven legs." He spins on his heels, drops into the splits, and pops back up.

I wince. Just watching him makes my body hurt more. "Wait." I stare at Random. "It's voluntary, right? The dance thing?"

"Almost always." He winks.

CHAPTER SEVEN

"DON'T WORRY." Les leads the way out of Ops. "They know I'm short staffed this leg, so they wouldn't dare draft you for the comp." She glares, as if daring *them* to try to recruit me. Then her eyes widen in apparent horror. "You don't have any dance experience, do you?"

"You mean performing?" I gulp. "Nope, not gonna happen."

Ollie slides up beside me and gives a little wave before turning right and speeding away. Les waves back and turns to the left.

"Ollie's probably headed to the gym. If you want to work out the kinks after a shift, I can take you there tomorrow. Most of us hit it after a long shift." She leans in close. "There's a hot tub and a steam room."

I smile. "That sounds like my kind of gym. My roommate is always trying to get me to work out, but it's just so much effort."

Les laughs. "Trust me, if you don't start now, you're going to wish you had when you get older. Come on, I'll take you to your berth."

We take a float tube up one level and walk down the corridor, the pins and needles in my leg finally fading. I shift my bag to my other shoulder and roll my neck. Les explains the layout of the ship.

"Obviously, the back, or stern, of the ship is reserved for the thrusters. The rest of the ship is modeled on ocean going ship design, stupid as that is! The lower decks of the ship, 'below the waterline,' are ship operations, maintenance, fuel storage, kitchens, cargo, and crew quarters. The upper decks are for passengers. Over the years, different cruise lines have tried changing that layout, but the passengers won't book rooms below G Deck. It's crazy."

"Sounds like the station." I shift my bag back again. "Lower levels are for the station crew and employees. The wealthy folks live in the upper levels. Which is ridiculous, because most of the levels are pretty interchangeable, design wise."

"Way above my pay grade. I leave that to the marketing gurus. Here we are." She gestures to a door marked C-251. "Crew dining is on B, or you can have bot-delivery. We also have our own gym down on B. When you're off duty, you can frequent the passenger areas, but only on a space-available basis, and you must be in uniform. If you're asked to leave, it means the venue is filling up. If you're eating, they'll pack your food and send it down to your berth. Meals are provided, but you get assessed a surcharge if you use the passenger dining. You don't get charged if you're bumped. In fact, some of the crew like to pick the most expensive restaurants at the busiest times, in hopes of getting a free meal." She smiles, then glances around. "Management frowns on that, of course.

"You have access to guides in your holo-file. Just click the location you want, and the guide will lead you there. You'll also find your work schedule, a catalog of all available vids, schedules for the various venues on the ship. We have theaters, spas, shopping, restaurants, sports teams, bars, pretty much anything you'd find on a station like yours. Let me know if you have any problems. Oh, and some of us have a little party on the second night out. Departure night is usually pretty busy, so we're ready to relax. I'll send you a link to the location."

"I—thanks."

"Come down to the gym after you settle in, if you want." She claps me on the shoulder and swings away. "Welcome aboard!"

"Thanks," I say again, but she's gone. I turn and wave my holo-ring at the door plate. The door slides open, and low lights come on. Squinting into the dark room, I step inside and the door whooshes closed behind me.

"Turn off the lights," a deep voice growls. "I have to get up in five hours." A pillow flies out of the dark and lands at my feet. Apparently, I have a roommate who works the night shift. The room is small, with dim lights in the ceiling panels. My eyes gradually adjust, and I can almost make out the tiny space.

"You have got to be kidding me!" Three bunks are stacked into each side wall, with privacy-slides to block the light. No one bothered to mention I'd be sharing my room with five other people!

"Shut it!" the helpful voice snaps. That's fair, I made noise. But if he has his p-slide set correctly, it blocks out the light and noise. Which means he just likes to be annoyed. Perfect.

I flick on the low-light setting on my holo-ring and open the files Les mentioned. The one marked *quarters* tells me I'll be sleeping in the middle bunk on the right. I step closer, ignoring the angry muttering from bottom left. Two slim drawers provide storage in the bunk supporting my bed. A card stuck to the front of one has my name and ship ID number printed in black.

Inside the bunk, the bed is made up, but the pillow is missing. I look at the one by the door, then lean over to snag it and toss it on my bed. A shelf runs across the foot of the bunk, giving the occupant space for a few small personal items. An adjustable light sticks out from the headboard. There should be just enough room for me to sit up in the bunk. I wonder how Ollie—a sizable man even without legs—tolerates living like this.

"Turn off the *pork chop* light!" the voice snarls.

I spin around, but the bunk slide is opaqued. "Sorry," I say, not sounding very sorry at all. I heave my bag up onto my bunk and set the p-slide to lock. "You should report that malfunctioning p-slide to maintenance." I wave the door open and escape before he can reply.

Outside the cabin, I call O'Neill.

"Hey! Where are you?" His voice is barely audible over the wash of noise. It sounds like a party.

"I'm outside my berth. Where are you?"

"Departure party! Come on up!" The call disconnects.

Seriously? He's too busy partying to talk to me?

I pull up the ship schedule. Departure parties are raging in the Solar-Deck, the StarDeck, the Embarkation Lobby, the Stardust Dining Room, and every bar in between. So helpful, O'Neill.

Using my staff access, I log in to the operating system and locate O'Neill's holo-ring. He's in the StarDeck, a huge compartment at the front of the ship on the top deck. I tag him and set my holo-ring to track him down. The pull on my finger takes me to the left.

I wander up several decks and reach an area where the carpet is plusher, the furniture more expensive looking. I pass a multi-gravity sports arena, a couple theaters, a child-care facility, a spa, and more bars and lounges than I can count. Stylishly dressed people stroll along, looking down their noses at my creased clothing.

Eventually, I make my way to the front of the ship and right up to the top deck. A holo casts the words "StarDeck" in three-dimensional, meter-high, glittering, silver letters, dancing and shimmying across a wide dark opening. My ring tugs me forward, so I step through the lightshow into the darkness.

As soon as I break the plane of the sign, the StarDeck assaults my eyes, ears, and nose. Hundreds of formally dressed passengers sit, lounge, stroll and dance throughout an enormous space. Small tables mark the edge of a shiny dance floor. A band plays in the corner to my right, swinging through a jazzy, bubbly number. White-coated waiters whisk through the crowds, offering sweet and savory snacks and beverages, and spiriting away dirty plates and glasses.

The ceiling is a huge, transparent dome. Most of the dome shines with thousands of stars. On the right, Station Kelly-Kornienko anchors us in place, slowly spinning us away from the sun. Once we reach the optimum launch angle, the access arms will release their clamps and the tug-bots will nudge us away from the station.

I glance quickly at the station, mentally bidding farewell to my home. Then I follow the tug of my ring across the room. I dodge a couple doing a wildly energetic dance in the middle of the floor. They smile widely, their eyes twinkling, their hair bouncing, their arms and legs kicking and spinning. The man makes eye contact with me and gives me a glare, mouthing "get off the floor!" Then the smile snaps back into place.

Glancing around, I realize I've wandered right into to the middle of a performance. I scramble to the left and between the tables at the edge of the dance floor. Dodging past a chair, I trip over a passenger's foot and barely catch my balance. An arm snakes out and pulls me down.

"Look what I caught!" a voice crows. A round of laughter answers.

I'm sitting on a tall, thin man's lap. His green hair is spiked into six-centimeter spires all over his head. He looks like a porcupine. Smooth, young skin surrounds eyes that look old enough to have seen the exodus from Earth. They're cold gray, hard and calculating.

I leap to my feet, pulling free from his arm. "Sorry, ser. I must have tripped." Over his carefully placed leg, I don't add. I know this type. He's wealthy—has to be to afford this ship and that kind of esthetic modification—and used to getting what he wants. Accusing him of anything will land me in more trouble than it's worth.

His table-mates laugh again, and one slaps me on the butt as I scramble away. I grit my teeth and focus on the pull of the ring, being careful to watch my feet. Drunken top-levs. Just what I don't need.

I scoot around a few more tables, ducking away from waiters with heavily laden trays. I don't need any more attention than I've already gotten. The ring pulses quickly, and I glance up.

There he is, leaning casually against the back of a plush sofa. And boy, is he shiny in his formal *tux-i-doo*. The dark coat sports a satiny stand-up collar that frames his strong jaw. His dark hair, just long enough to brush the top of his shirt collar, waves softly over his ears. His chocolate brown eyes are surrounded by thick, dark lashes that I would have to endure hours in an ehood to attain. For a second, I just stand there and drink in his perfection. Then I notice his companion.

He's smiling at a brunette in an extremely tight, green gown. Her breasts bulge above the top of the strapless bodice, making me wonder what is keeping them inside the dress. The neckline plunges to her navel, and the wide skirt is split in the front, allowing her to show off spectacular legs and blindingly bright silver stilettos. A hint of what I *hope* is sparkling panties peeks out at the top of the split in the skirt.

As if he feels the weight of my stare, O'Neill turns and spots me. His smile amps up in a way that makes me feel like the prettiest girl in the room. I try not to grin, but a smile twitches at my lips and spreads across my face.

"Hey," I say.

The woman turns, spots me, and holds out her empty glass. "Bring me another gargle blaster." She lets go of the glass as she turns back to Ty.

If she'd asked, I could have told her that was a bad idea. Even if I'd tried to catch it, I would have missed—I'm kind of clumsy. Especially when I want to be. The glass shatters against the shining tiles of the floor, and people standing around turn to look.

"Oh, dear, you dropped something." I point, covering my smile with my other hand.

O'Neill's lips twitch, but he holds it together. The brunette barely glances at me. "Clean that up!"

"Do I look like I'm wearing a waiter's uniform?" I ask.

She turns and gives me a once-over from the top of my messy red hair to the soles of my worn shoes. "My mistake." Her eyes glint icily. "The staff here are much better dressed."

O'Neill flicks a waiter call signal on his holo-ring and turns to me. "We should probably go." He gives the brunette his best schmoozing smile. "It was delightful to meet you, Lady Grandelle. I hope to see you later in the cruise."

She cranks up her perfect, million-credit smile, but he turns away and ushers me towards the door. "Since you actually are staff," he whispers, "you might not want to piss off the paying customers."

I narrow my eyes. "I am NOT wait staff."

"I doubt Lady Grandelle would care. She's the 'get 'em fired first, ask questions later type." He places a hand on the small of my back and urges me across the room.

CHAPTER EIGHT

A VOICE BOOMS out over the speakers and through my internal audio implant. "The CSS Morningstar will depart Station Kelly-Kornienko in ten seconds! Nine, eight..."

The crowd takes up the chant, "Seven, Six, Five..."

We step through the door, and quiet falls like a blanket. Even the audio implant is silent. "Is there a way to mute that voice?" I rub the back of my ear. "I really didn't need it through the internal audio."

"Didn't you watch the pre-departure info vid?" O'Neill directs me toward the float tubes.

"When would I have done that? I've been working since I got on-board at oh-dark-thirty today."

We take a float tube down two floors, and he guides me around a corner and toward the front of the ship.

At the end of the hallway, a door marked "Maia Suite" slides open at his wave. We step inside and I gasp. This suite occupies the front right corner of the deck. Floor-to-ceiling transparent aluminum walls provide an amazing view as the ship slowly peels away from the SK2 docking arm, headed out to deep space.

Well, not really. We're headed to the jump belt. Like the official jump belts in all mapped systems, it is located 'south' of the sun, at roughly one astronomical unit. Since in-system traffic stays pretty close to the plane of the planetary orbits, jump belts are set out of the way: inbound traffic north of the primary, outbound to the south, at least 45 degrees from the planetary plane. The ship's speed and distance from the sun impact the destination. There are mathematical formulae that dictate where and how you'll jump back out, but I get flashbacks to seventh grade math when I think about it:

If Ship A departs the Grissom orbital plane at an angle of 29 degrees and speed 0.8C, and Ship B departs at an angle of 35 degrees and speed 0.57C, which ship will reach Sally Ride first?

Makes me shudder, just thinking about it. I prefer to have the computer do the calculating.

Cruise ships generally take the leisurely approach, taking a day or two to reach jump, then another couple days to the next station. Freighters use steeper angles to increase their range. Military ships are built to withstand higher Gs and can dive closer to the sun to increase their speed and distance.

Regardless, the sight of departing the station is pretty spectacular. The station rotates away just as the planet, Kaku, comes into view. We sail by, enjoying a last look at the purple, green and white swirls before it, too, wheels out of sight.

I take a deep breath of vanilla-scented air and survey the room. The obnoxious peach, maroon and lime green color scheme of the Pleiades Star-Cruises is gone. This suite is done in subtle earth tones. A thick, dark brown carpet stretches across the deck. Glossy champagne and cream striped linen covers the walls, and plush brown Lether couches face the wide wall of windows. Bookshelves and cupboards of mellow blond synth-wood fill the wall by the door, providing space for an AutoKich'n, vases of fresh flowers, and a silver wine chiller. Through a partially open door, I can see a thick bed with about a hundred pillows.

It's a far cry from my cramped bunk.

"Is it too late to change my mind about this trip?" I ask.

O'Neill hands me a plate of nachos. This man knows the way to a girl's heart. "Since we just left the station, I think so. But why would you want to change your mind? This place is pretty fantastic."

“Haven’t you been on a cruise before?”

“When would I have done that?” He drops down into the couch and pats the seat beside him. “I went to the Academy, then got a job on the station. The only vacations I’ve taken have been dirtside on Kaku. I haven’t been able to take enough time off to make the long trip back to Grissom to see my family.”

“That’s kind of sad,” I say, knowing his family is very close. “Maybe you can make the swing through on the way back to SK2?”

“We’ll see how this trip goes.” He looks away. “Why do you want to change your mind?”

“Have you seen the crew quarters on this tub?” I shovel down a couple nachos—I’m starving. “I have a two-meter square bunk, in a compartment shared with five other grunts. I’ve only met one of my roommates so far and let’s just say he isn’t winning any prizes for congeniality.”

“Well, at least you don't have to hot-bunk.” O’Neill snags one of my chips.

I do a double take. “Hot bunk? You mean share with someone on a different shift? Zark! I hope not.” Frantically, I pull up my contract and page through to the accommodations section. Nope, no bunk sharing. It’s specifically called out in the contract, so this must be standard on some ships. Yikes.

“You can always bunk in with me.” O’Neill gives me an exaggerated leer. “But seriously, I have plenty of room.”

“I’m not sure that would be allowed. The standards for employees are pretty strict. I don’t want to get fired.” Although, on second thought, getting fired might be an excellent option. I’ll have to look into the ramifications.

“If you’re going to stay on the payroll here, you might want to be more careful around the passengers. Lady Grandelle does not seem like the forgiving type.” O’Neill gets to his feet. “Of course, you can stay here if things get hairy. I’ll see if I can give you access to the suite.”

“Don’t bother.” I struggle out of the deep couch. “You know me. I can get in anywhere. I might have trouble explaining why I don’t leave, though, if anyone checks the records.”

“Are you allowed to go to dinner with me, or do we need to order in? I know you'll want to eat, and we might want to make plans for the rest of the cruise."

We end up ordering in. I just can't face whatever red-tape will be required to eat in a passenger space, and now that I've seen the revelers in the Star-Deck, I know my clothing would stick out like a sore thumb. The CSS Morningstar lives up to its reputation and delivers a fabulous pizza and some sparkling drinks to wash it down with.

Once we've eaten half the pie, I sit back. "I'm working twelve-hour days," I tell O'Neill. "Straight through to S'Ride. The good news is, I get a huge overtime bonus. But I won't have a lot of free time. I hope you'll be able to keep yourself occupied."

O'Neill points to a stack of printed materials on the side table. "Have you seen the schedules for this place? Fitness classes, sports teams, short courses in culinary, technology, astronomy, astrology, wine tasting, photography, painting, pretty much anything you might want to learn to do. With no homework. Then there are movies, virtual reality games, live theater, music, meditation. I don't think keeping busy will be a problem."

"Well, I guess we can plan on meeting in the evenings, after dinner? I can go to the passenger restaurants, but risk getting bumped. And I'm not sure how they feel about the help hanging out with passengers."

"Evenings might be a problem for me," O'Neill admits. Is he blushing?

"Why is that? You were just bragging about how much free time you'll have."

His face is definitely red. "I'm signed up for a dance competition. Apparently, it's a thing on this ship."

"You're doing the dance thing?" I laugh. "How did you get roped into that?"

He looks defensive. "I enjoy dancing, believe it or not. When Ambar asked me, I was flattered."

"Ambar? The Techno-Inst intern?" I stare at him, open-mouthed. "How do you know her?"

"I don't." He takes a swig of his cider and shrugs. "The pre-cruise vid allows you to indicate your interests, and I selected rock climbing and dancing. Then I got an intra-ship call from a staff member, asking if I wanted to participate. They offered to let me choose a partner, but I told them to just match me up with someone. Ambar sent me a pairing request."

I'll just bet she did. Based on my trek through the ship, young and handsome is in short supply here. Ambar must have kept a pretty sharp eye on the possible partners list. You have to hand it to the girl—she dialed in to the system pretty quickly. I would have expected one of the old hands—like Kindra—to have snapped up a specimen like O'Neill.

"We'll be practicing every evening this leg, with the competition on the last night before we make S'Ride."

"Every night? Can't you practice during the day? Instead of all the wine tasting and Pilates classes?" I finish my own drink and push the glass aside.

"Ambar works the day shift, so she booked the studio for two hours each night. But early, from seven to nine. Plenty of time to shower and change before the late dinner seating. People are up pretty late on the ship. The entertainment doesn't really get going until after ten." He picks up our glasses and stacks them into the cafe-bot.

"People may be up late here, but staff are not. At least this staff is not. I am exhausted." I push my chair away from the table. "Are you practicing tonight?"

"No, we start tomorrow. Ambar was busy with departure night festivities."

Well good for Ambar. I yawn. "Whatever. I'm going to bed."

"I have a really comfortable bed," O'Neill says, hopefully.

"Good for you," I grump. "Maybe Ambar will test it out for you."

O'Neill narrows his eyes at me. "What's up with you tonight?"

I shake my head. "I just worked a twelve-hour shift, learning a new system. I'm tired. I'll talk to you tomorrow." I run away before I can say anything stupid. Or stupider.

MY ALARM CHIMES through my audio implant, waking me with the pop tune *A Good Day Ain't Got No Drama.* I grab my holo-ring from its charging station and slide it on, flicking the silence button as soon as it pops up. The song stops mid word. I really need to find something new; that one is getting on my last nerve.

When I switch off my p-slide, the sounds of activity filter in from the room. I push it open. Two women are dressing. A tall thin woman with silver and green hair yanks her top off and tosses it into the top bunk on the opposite side. Muscles ripple across her narrow shoulders, but her bony spine protrudes down the center. The other woman is short and round, with mousy brown hair and big eyes.

"Good morning!" The shorter woman spots me and waves. "Come on down! I'm Maarta. Dining services."

The green-haired woman turns and flashes a smile. Her bare chest is as bony as her back, and she is completely blasé about her lack of clothing. "I'm Simean. Call me Sim. Propulsion."

The bottom left bunk is empty, thankfully.

I glance down to make sure the space below me is clear. Swinging my legs out into the room, I drop to the floor. Carefully not looking at Sim's chest, I bump fists with each of the women. "I'm Triana, temp in Maintenance."

Sim grins at me again and drops her pants. Now completely naked, she steps up onto the bottom left bunk and climbs up the middle one like a ladder. She stretches into the top bunk, rummaging around the shelf at the foot. Her bare butt is less than an arm's-length from my face.

Maarta glances at me and laughs. "Sim, put some clothes on! You're scaring the new girl."

I stutter, but Maarta waves me off. "Sim's a bit of an exhibitionist. She loves to fluster newbies. The crew here are generally pretty casual about privacy—we have to be the way they have us slotted in here like memory cards—but Sim likes to take it up a notch just to get a rise. Pun intended." She laughs again.

Sim groans. "Every time!"

"Hey, if you're going to drop your pants every time we get a new roommate, I'm going to use the same pun."

Sim grabs a basket from her bunk shelf, and a handful of clothing from the drawer underneath. "I'm hitting the shower." She struts across the room and into the tiny sonic booth.

"Close your mouth," Maarta says cheerfully. "Sim grew up in a nudist colony on Gagarin. Once she realized the rest of the galaxy wasn't as free with their bodies, it became a game to her. The sooner you stop reacting, the sooner we can all stop getting an eye-full of her bony ass." She laughs again. I'm getting the idea she laughs a lot.

"I gotta run—I'm training a new staff-member and have to babysit a couple interns." She rolls her eyes. "They are way more trouble than they're worth!" She slaps a magnetic name tag to her uniform. "If no one else has mentioned it, there's a party in the staff dining hall tonight. Come along any time after 8pm. We'll all be there." She waves and disappears out the door.

CHAPTER NINE

WHEN SIM STEPS OUT of the shower booth, I'm leaning against the wall, buck naked with my toiletries and a towel in hand. No nudist is going to fluster me more than once. I don't know what I would have done if one of our other roommates had come in while I was waiting.

Sim gives me a quick up and down glance and a twisted grin. "You're going to be okay."

I grin back and head to the shower.

By the time I'm done with my allotted five minutes, the cabin is empty. I sigh in relief. I prefer to keep my skin covered in company, so hopefully my preemptive strike will ward off any future required exhibitions.

I pull my uniform from the drawer under my bunk. Lime green coverall with peach and maroon piping. I'm not much of a fashionista, but even I can tell this is hideous. I grit my teeth and step into the clothing.

As I stride down the corridor towards Ops, Ollie zips up beside me. His device is so quiet, I didn't even hear him. He's at standing height as he skims down the hall, and he gives me a little finger wave.

"How's it going, Ollie?"

"Can't complain," he says. "Got a new move."

Before I can ask what he means, he grabs my hand and spins me away. Then, with a flick of his arm, he spins me back in toward him. His device whines a little, as the hover servos strain to keep up, and he whirls me through three spins before catching me in a dip. Then he whips me up and sends me back to my starting point.

"Seriously?" I sputter. "Is everyone on this ship obsessed with dancing?"

"Why else would you work here?"

"I thought it was for the sandwiches?"

The Ops door slides open. A techno-jazz dance band blares out into the hall at a volume nothing short of an atmo-rocket trying to escape a high-g world. Ollie hands me something. The package says SuperDens Ear Guard. Gratefully, I rip it open and shove the foamy bits into my ears.

Inside, Random and Kindra demonstrate the dance contest is definitely why *they* work here. As I walk in, Kindra is high in the air, her legs kicked up behind, skirt and hair flying. She swings gracefully down, landing lightly on the balls of her feet, spinning around Random. Not to be outdone, he executes a gravity defying backflip. He swings around and spins Kindra in close to his chest.

Kindra flings an arm out in a jerky motion, and the music stops. "No! No! No! The sedric link comes before the astral spin! Why can't you get that right?!" She jerks away from him, glaring.

Random draws himself up to his full meter and a half height, his dark eyes flashing. "I am the leader. You respond to my lead! It doesn't matter what you think should happen, I am in charge. You are merely the choreographer!"

Ollie slides between the two. "Morning."

I slowly pull the SuperDens out of my ears. "Good morning," I say, uncertainly.

Random rotates smoothly toward me and bows. "Good morning, lovely Triana. I'm so sorry you had to witness that." He flicks a venomous glance at Kindra.

"I'm leading, next time," she spits back at him. Then she turns to me. "Good morning Triana! I hope you're ready for a busy day!" Her voice carries no hint of the anger she just spewed at Random. She spins back toward her desk. With a few waves and flicks, she logs out and the screens go dark. "It's all yours!"

She and Random link arms and stroll out of the room.

I look at Ollie. "Is that normal?"

He shrugs and slides into his workstation. I guess he used up all his words for the day. And it's only six am.

I log in to the system and page after page of red, blinking alerts scroll up in front of me. "What the fork?" I freeze. Back on SK2, I'd get my pay docked for saying "fork" in that tone of voice, but either the ship OS has different standards, or the system hasn't identified my pet swear word yet. Probably the latter. "Didn't they do anything last night?"

"Can't enter staterooms if they're occupied," Ollie says.

"But don't people stay out partying late on this ship?" I saw enough of them staggering around last night, but I went to bed pretty early. I click on the first ticket, from 9:16 last night. Faulty plumbing. Bots deployed. Toilet unclogged. "The bots corrected this issue—why is it still showing red?"

Ollie shrugs again. "Kindra must have missed it."

My eyes narrow, and I look through the next few alerts. Most of these should have been confirmed once the bot completed the work. I scroll down the list. Plumbing problems, spilled food, broken glass, missing towels, lost luggage. "Most of these are housekeeping problems."

The door slides open and Les walks in. "I'm filling in for the junior purser today, so you two are on your own," she announces. She glances at my screen, then strides over to me. "Ollie, why didn't you tell her how to deal with this stuff?" Ollie ignores her.

Les flicks an icon at the top of the list, waves a hand through the red print and swipes to the right. A whole page of the red print turns green and slides out of sight. She shows me the sequence again, eliminating another forty items. "If it isn't flashing, it's good. Kindra's terrible about clearing the docket."

"You mean we don't have to check those? We just assume they were repaired?" This is completely foreign to my experience on SK2. We double check everything.

"The bots are good, and most of those things are minor anyway. The cabin stewards will get a call if the fix didn't work, so we just clear them and move on. It's the flashing ones you need to worry about."

"I could write a code slip to do that automatically," I say.

Ollie's head snaps around, and he shakes it, eyes wide.

"What?" Les demands. "You can't do that—we have to check them manually."

"But you didn't." Behind her Ollie shakes his head again, sadly this time, and turns back to his work.

Les draws herself up. "The records will show I checked each of those tickets. Anyone who says differently is either incorrect or unfamiliar with the protocol here." She gives me a hard stare. "We follow the protocol. Perhaps you'd better familiarize yourself with it." She flicks an icon, and a text file opens on my screen.

Les stalks out of the room without another word. Ollie waves as she passes him, but he doesn't look up from his work.

After the door shuts, he cocks his head at me. "Don't question Les. She don't like it."

"Thanks for the advice, Ollie." I roll my eyes and start swiping red tickets.

Scrolling through the red lines, I swipe angrily. This is not how we do business on SK2, but if that's what they do here, I'm game. I build a virtual corral, and swipe all Kindra's red tickets into it, hiding them from my view. Now I can focus on the real problems.

I wish I hadn't. The first flashing red line is a clogged toilet that the bot has not been able to clear. I consult Les' precious manual and key in a call to the steward in charge of that deck.

"Yah?"

"Uh, Maintenance," I reply, flustered by the very unprofessional response. "The bots report an unresolved situation in cabin 104."

"Yeah, what are you waiting for? Come up and fix it!" The line goes dead.

I turn and look at Ollie. "Just what is the deal here? The manual says to check in with the steward. But he seems to think I should have just come up to deal with it."

Ollie shakes his head slowly. "Wait."

I level a look at him. "For what?"

"Who blinks first."

"Are you kidding me? We play chicken with Housekeeping?" I rub a hand over my eyes.

Ollie gives me his usual thumbs up.

Fan-forking-tastic.

A neon yellow telltale on my board flashes. I flick the icon. "Maintenance, Moore."

A dark face pops into view. "You gonna fix this crapper, or what?"

I glance at Ollie. "Sorry, we're swamped here. Minor issue in navigation. I'll have to get back to you." I disconnect.

Ollie grins and winks. "Nice. Don't trot that one out too often, though."

"I guess I'll have to come up with a list of excuses." I start working my way through the flashing list, palming off the problems onto the staff members who posted the ticket. I'm not plunging toilets because the stewards are too lazy to do it themselves.

A few things, I can't get out of. I spend ninety minutes reprogramming the professional grade Autokich'n on G Deck, tweaking some nanobots for the ship's doc to use on a passenger who twisted a leg in the multi-grav gym, and rerouting the cleaning bots to avoid an unscheduled party in the Solar-Deck. About an hour before the end of my shift, I find myself up in the Rio Dining Room.

"The vacu-bot ran over your toes?" I say, disbelieving.

Ambar sneers at me, rubbing her foot. "I was setting up the tables, and your bot just slammed into me!"

I look down at the crumpled bot. It looks like an elephant stomped on it. "How did it get this huge dent in the top?"

Ambar flutters her eyes. "I don't know." Faux innocence drips from her words.

"You know these bots have cams on them, right?" I pop a holo up in my palm. How could she not know?

Ambar's face blanches. "I, I…"

"Save it." I stretch the vid to almost life sized. The cam shows a 360-degree view around us, as if we're the bot. It slides along the floor between the tables, and out of nowhere, a foot slams down.

I glance down at Ambar's bright green shoes. "Why?"

Ambar raises her chin. "They match the trim." She runs a defensive hand over the green piping on her peach jacket.

I roll my eyes. "Not the color—why did you stomp on my bot?"

"I didn't know it was yours," she pouts. "It was everywhere. Zipping around the room like a self-important little, uh..."

"Vacu-bot?"

"Look, I'm having a really bad day! I came in third yesterday, behind Arstend and Steve! *Steve!* I cannot lose to Steve!"

"Well, I don't know why you'd take your anger out on my bot." I crouch down and pop the cover off the little bot. "Don't worry, little bot, I'll take care of you," I whisper.

"What are you, some kind of bot-whisperer?" Ambar flounces away to the next table, pushing a little cart of silverware.

"I am *the* bot-whisperer." I type in some commands and send the bot back to the garage. It limps away, damaged, but mobile. Flicking through some icons, I activate some repair bots and leave them waiting for the damaged one. "I thought you were wearing a body cam? Aren't you worried this will lose you more points for today?"

Ambar's face goes even paler. She drops into a chair and bursts into tears. Perfect.

I heave a sigh and drop down beside her. "Why don't you tell me what the problem is?"

Ambar's shoulders shake, and she bawls. I awkwardly pat her back. "Look, just stop crying and tell me what's going on."

After a few minutes, I hand her a napkin from one of the tables. She blows her nose and tries to hand it back to me. I hold up my hands to ward it off. "You keep that. Or better, put it into the laundry bot." I flick my holo-ring, and a bot zips in from the butler's pantry. The hatch pops open. Ambar wipes her eyes and blows her nose again, then drops the napkin into the bot. It zips away.

"This morning, we had to design center-pieces from a pile of junk!" She pulls up a vid and flicks it to me.

"I thought you were supposed to be a steward?" The vid starts playing. Ambar, Steve, Arstend and Zibia stand in the center of a room that is pretty much identical to this one. The only difference I can see is the color of the carpet, which is peach rather than maroon.

"I was!" she wails. "But that *spiced olive* Frankl put me into dining services, thanks to you!"

"So, you stomped on my bot?"

On the vid, Ambar and Zibia are fighting over a piece of curved, shiny something. In the background, Arstend and Steve paw through the items on the table, whispering together and putting pieces aside.

She grinds her teeth. "I didn't know it was your *pistachio* bot. I'm just so *prime rib* frustrated!" She leaps out of her chair, kicking it over. "I was the top of my class at the Techno-Inst. And now I'm behind Steve. *Steve*! Aaar-rrgh!" She yanks a tablecloth off the nearest table. She's obviously going for maximum destruction. The plates and glasses wobble frantically, but stay in place, like props in a magic show. Ambar yells again and raises an arm to sweep the table clean.

I leap up and grab her wrist. "Don't." I twist her arm around behind her and spin her around. "I don't want to have to send a sweep bot up here, especially since you'll probably damage it too. Get your temper under control, or they'll send you back to Kaku in a rescue pod."

Ambar freezes, her eyes wide. "They will?"

"I would," I say, bluntly. Well, I'd want to, but it's against the rules. Probably. More importantly, there would be a lot of overrides to work through, and my common sense would kick in before I got that far. I let go of her arm.

Ambar slumps down in her chair. "Whatever. Go away."

"Fine." I turn away. "Don't kick my bots."

Ambar growls, but the fight has gone out of her. I head for the door. Just outside, a familiar woman in a peach jacket with two rows of lime green trim on each sleeve grins at me. "That will make for some excellent viewing."

"What?" I stare at the woman. Her name tag reads Watkins—the assistant purser who babysat the interns yesterday.

"For the reality show." She peers at her palm. I look down and see a feed of the dining room, with Ambar slumped on the table, crying. The word "live" flashes green at the top of the feed.

"Reality show? Like on *Ancient TēVē*? You have got to be kidding me! Do they know?" I jerk a thumb back at the door.

"It was in the contract they signed." She shrugs and walks away.

I rub my temple, feeling a headache coming on.

CHAPTER TEN

WHEN KINDRA ARRIVES THAT EVENING, I'm ready. I've completed all my flashing tickets and cleared them from the board. The redlined items she left for me are back in the bin, waiting for her clearance. I don't mind working hard, but I'm not doing someone else's cleanup.

"Hard night of dancing ahead?" I ask as she and Random stroll in, ten minutes late.

Random strikes a pose, but Kindra gives me a considering look, then an arch smile. "I take night shift for a reason," she says.

I log out of my console and shift it down to the neutral position. Ollie glides out of his, and Random and Kindra log in. I hear her angry intake of breath just as I reach the door. Turning, I smile blandly. "Everything okay?"

Kindra shakes back her startling hair and lifts her chin. She gives me a once-over that would have made me feel like dirt if I hadn't been raised by the Ice Dame. I stare back, my face showing regal unconcern. My decorum teacher would have been proud.

She glances at the screen again, then smiles, as if acknowledging something. "It's all good, honey."

Random looks from me to Kindra and back again. When Kindra turns away, he winks. Ollie and I glide out into the corridor.

Well, Ollie glides. I trip on the threshold, and he catches me before I can smack my chin against the wall. I glance back, but the door has shut behind us.

"She didn't see," Ollie says. "Gym?"

"Thanks, but not tonight. I think I got in enough steps today." I wince, glancing at his hover device.

Ollie catches my eye and grins. "Not me! Good work, today." He takes my hand, twirls me around, and zips away.

I stand in the hallway, considering my options. I can change my mind and follow Ollie to the gym. Yuck. I can go back to my bunk and take a nap, except Ser Cranky Bottom Left will likely be there. Maybe I can figure out a way to automatically engage his p-slide when he's in the bunk. I set that problem to simmer in the back of my brain.

I can hit the crew dining hall and grab a snack—never a bad idea in my mind—or wait until the party tonight. Or I can go watch Ambar and Ty at their dance practice. Decisions, decisions.

I swing by the crew chow hall and snag a couple brownies, an apple, and a bottle of juice, then set my holo-ring to find O'Neill. It takes me up to I Deck, and forward about halfway along the ship. On the right, an endless line of closed cabin doors stretches off into the distance. On my left, every half-dozen cabins is interrupted by a door marked Studio. My ring vibrates when I reach Studio I-14.

I lean against the wall and tuck my half-eaten brownie into my bag along with the other snacks. Flicking my holo-ring, I log into the ship OS and pull up the cam feeds from this deck. Cabins are off limits, of course, although I'm sure I could hack into one if I needed to. But the Studio I-14 cam is open to anyone with OS access.

Inside, O'Neill and Ambar stand in the middle of an empty floor. A slender woman with very short, silver-blonde hair demonstrates a move in front of the mirrored wall. Her movements are loose and fluid, but precise. I flick the image, and her name pops up: Joan Lesley, Dance Instructor.

"May I help you? Oh, it's you." One of the interns from Kaku—the swear-happy boy with the dark crew-cut—stands in front of me. "You're Technician Moore."

I hold out a fist. "Call me Triana. It's Tei Chaia, right?"

He grins. "Yeah. I go by TC. You sure pissed off Ambar."

I laugh. "Which time?"

He laughs with me. "You tangled with her again? I can't wait to hear about that." He gestures towards the studio door. "She's in there. Is that why you're lurking? Planning something else?"

Remembering the body cams, I hold up my hands. "Hey, I got nothing against Ambar. She likes to challenge people for no reason, but I don't do revenge. I'm actually here to see her partner. He's a friend of mine from SK2."

The boy smirks. "Just a friend? Does she know he's with you? You should have seen the way she jumped on the chance to dance with him. The second his pic popped up in the app, she was all over it. I don't know if she's looking for a fling with a hot guy, or if she thinks he'll be a good addition to her network." He glances at my holo. "Why don't you go over to Studio I-15? It's on the other side of this one, with a programmable window between. Come on, I'll show you."

"Don't you have to work?" I follow him down the hall and through a cross corridor.

"I drew the day shift. Brett is working the night. He's my assigned mentor. They like to start the interns on the day when there's fewer passengers in the rooms." TC flicks his holo and the door to Studio I-15 slides open. We step in, and he flicks a few icons in his palm. The mirrored wall across from the door clears and becomes floor-to-ceiling windows.

"They're one-way right now." Opening a cupboard door, TC pulls out a couple folding chairs and plops them into the middle of the floor. "You had dinner?"

I drop into one of the surprisingly comfortable chairs. "I grabbed some snacks, but I didn't want to hang out in the chow hall on my own." I pull the brownies out of my bag and offer him one.

TC settles into the other chair and takes a brownie. "I know what you mean. It's like high school, all over again. Where do I sit? Who are the popular kids? Why are they staring at me?" He takes a bite and sighs happily. "I'd much rather sit here and watch that."

That is Ambar trying to master a body roll. She thrusts her bony shoulders one way, and her well-padded derriere the other. Her elbows fly out, her knees bend, and her hips swing.

"She looks like she's having convulsions!" TC hoots.

I wince. "It does look painful."

"Hey, that brownie was good. You got any more?" The boy flicks his holo-ring and calls up a menu. "I'm starving. Let's order some food." He flicks some commands and closes the screen without asking what I want.

We settle back into our chairs and watch the show. Ambar gives up on the body roll, and stalks over to the mirror to check her eye makeup. TC giggles and jumps up. He runs up to the window and stares through the glass, making faces at Ambar. When she pulls her lips back to check her teeth, he howls with laughter.

"Aren't you worried about the body cam?" I ask.

"You mean this?" He turns away from the glass and pulls a flat silver packet out of his pocket. "I read my contract after you clued us in to the swearing thing. We're required to wear these when we're on duty, but not during our off-hours. I figure if they've got a cam, they've got a mic, so I wrapped mine in a privacy foil at the end of the shift. Ambar wears hers all the time. She seems to think she'll score better if she lets them have free reign to her life." He drops the device into his pocket, shaking his head.

Smartest of the bunch, I'd say. "Of course, these rooms are probably observed, too."

He smiles. "I disabled it when we came in."

I flick my holo-ring to life and sift through the system. The cam for studio I-15 is paused. A boy after my own heart. "I like you. Where'd you learn to hack like that?"

He grins and drops back into his seat. "This is my second year at the Techno-Inst. I started in coding but transferred to hospitality over the summer. I like people better than computers. But I know a few tricks."

"More than a few, I'd say." I turn as the door opens and a food bot scoots in. TC opens the top and reaches inside. The bot settles to the floor. "What did you do to it?"

"I turned the bot off. They're actually designed to be used as portable tables." He folds the door on either side up and flips a couple supports into place, then starts pulling dishes out of the bot to stack on top. "Scoot up and have some dinner."

I move my chair closer to the bot and glance at the dishes. They all have clear lids, with their contents clearly marked, and less clearly visible through the plastek covers. TC ordered nachos, pizza, bread sticks and some kind of cheesy dip, cookies, and more brownies. He and I must be related. We dig in.

Meanwhile, in the other room, the dance instruction continues. Ty stands in the center of the floor, chin up, arms out. He holds out a hand to Ambar. She takes his hand, and he gives a little pull. She spins in toward him, stumbling over her own feet then slamming into him. Ty staggers but stays upright.

TC laughs. "I think we need sound." He pulls up a screen on his holo and makes a few changes.

A deep but feminine voice rings through the room. "Chin up, shoulders down, Ambar. Maintain your frame!" The teacher pushes Ambar's face up and adjusts her arms. Ty and Ambar take three steps, and Ty trips over Ambar's leg. This time they both end up on the floor. Ambar bursts into tears.

I look at TC. "Seriously? That girl cries at the drop of a hat."

He smirks. "She thinks it's going to up her audience share. You know, sympathy for the underdog."

"Sympathy is not the emotion I'm feeling right now," I mutter. In fact, I'm feeling kind of grumpy. Maybe just a tad jealous. And kind of pissed off that she's going to make Ty look bad. "Do you really want to watch this? I think I can wait for the highlights show."

The window goes blank, and a series of vid ads swirl up. "We can watch a movie," TC says, hopefully.

"Don't you have better things to do with your time off? Hanging out with the other interns?"

He shrugs, looking a little forlorn. "They're all doing this dance thing. Or working the night shift. And the regular crew treat us like children. If I hadn't run into you, I'd be in my bunk, or blowing my paycheck on the slot machines." He mimes pulling a lever.

"We could go check out the gym..." What has happened to me? Those words have never crossed my lips before. "Or, there's a party later. Do you want to go with me?"

"A crew party?" His eyes grow big. "That would be stellar! The others would be so jealous!"

"Great," I lean forward to stack the empty dishes into the bot. "Let's get this cleaned up."

CHAPTER ELEVEN

TC GIVES me a tour of the ship. We peer into the StarDeck, where last night's party seems to be still going. Or maybe it's a new party; who can tell? We walk through the observation decks, the fitness centers, the multi-grav sports arena. We pass theaters, spas, restaurants, swimming pools, libraries, virtual shooting galleries, art displays, rock climbing walls, and shops. Row after row of high-end shops.

"This is the ice-skating track." We're standing in one of the observation decks, stars glittering around us. A transparent tube wraps around the ship, crossing the window at an angle. As we watch, a skater zips past, *up* the tube. "Localized gravity in those," TC says. "It feels flat, even though it looks slanted."

"That looks crazy risky, having that thing on the outside of a moving ship."

TC shrugs. "It's not really outside—just looks like it. Besides, cruise ships are pretty safe. They don't traverse asteroid fields or war-torn sectors."

"War-torn sectors? You've been watching too many action vids."

He shrugs again. "Whatever. Interstellar cruising is safer than crossing the street. Besides, they'd close the skate tubes, and the water slides, and the other 'external' areas if there were any danger. Evacuation practice was part of our first day of onboard training."

Further along, he shows me casinos, meeting rooms, childcare, art studios, and the virtual education center. "Some of the crew have kids, so the ship has to provide for their education. Can you imagine growing up on a cruiser? That would be awesome."

I spent a fair amount of time on cruisers as a kid, during some of Mother's longer business trips, and it's not as awesome as he thinks. For one thing, it's pretty lonely. Most of the kids you meet are only on board for a few days, then they leave again. Of course, if you keep in touch, you'd have contacts all over the galactic sector.

We grab a burger at one of the fast-food spots on H Deck, then head below. "Do you want to change before we go to the party?" I gesture to my creased, lime coverall.

"Good plan." TC grins, glancing down at his own maroon pants and peach shirt. "The ladies won't be very impressed with all this."

A snort escapes me. "Since most of them wear something similar all day, you're probably right. Where's your berth?"

"Steve and I have a cabin on F."

I stare at him. "You and Steve—just the two of you?"

"Yeah, why? Do you have more roommates?" He leads the way to the float tubes.

"I have *five* roommates. And one of them is really grumpy. Why do the interns have better quarters than the crew?" I pull up a ship diagram and filter out everything except crew quarters. The holo lights up, showing rooms scattered from the bottom deck up through F. There are a couple larger staterooms on higher decks designated for the captain and high-ranking crew. I zoom in on F deck. "Which room is yours?"

"F-36. There are four bunks, but two of them are empty."

Yup, F-36 shows a max occupancy of four, two currently assigned. "Maybe more interns will join the ship at S'Ride?"

TC shrugs. "Maybe. Shall I meet you at the chow hall, or find your cabin?"

"Come on down to C-251 when you're dressed." I wave and step into the float tube. I should have done more research before signing that contract. If they've only got half their complement of interns, I could have held out for an upgraded cabin.

Maarta and Sim are in the room when I get back. The bunk below Sim's is closed, but the other two are open.

"Did you know the interns are only two to a cabin?" I demand, not giving them a chance to say hello.

Sim blinks at me. "What?"

"Two?" Maarta looks around the cramped cabin. "They've crammed six of us in here, and the interns only have two?"

"That's what I said." I flick open the crew billet list and scroll through it, linking bunk assignments to rooms on the ship. Color coding the data, I stretch the holo so Sim and Maarta can see the ship schematic. "The colored rooms are crew quarters. The red ones have five or six people assigned. Yellows have three or four, and greens have only two." Most of the rooms are red, with a scattering of yellow, and a half-dozen greens.

"What are the blue?" Maarta waves toward a hallway lined with azure coded rooms.

I level a look at her. "Those are empty."

"What?!" Sim flings herself closer to the holo. "There are empty cabins? What the *basil?!*"

"The ship OS shows they're under renovation." I flick through some more files and pull up a listing. "But there's no record of any work being done. Maybe there's something wrong with them? They're all on the same corridor."

"I think we need to have a chat with the purser." Sim strips off her uniform coverall. She's naked underneath, of course. "He can explain why we're all crammed in here like data files."

Maarta turns her back to us and starts pulling off her uniform. "If we ask nicely, maybe they'll reassign us." She throws it hopefully over her shoulder.

I shrug and follow her example. Pulling on a green striped top, I rummage in my narrow drawer for a pair of leggings. "Or we can just help ourselves to the bounty."

Sim swings around, pants in hand. She has goosebumps all over her pale body. I throw a sweater at her. "Put some clothes on, Lady Godiva."

She catches the sweater and flings it back at me. "Lady Godiva? What does chocolate have to do with anything?"

"Chocolate is always relevant." I shove the sweater back into the crammed drawer. "But Lady Godiva was the first nudist. Or at least the first documented nudist. Seriously, shouldn't she be your patron saint or something?"

"Patrón saint? Is that a brand of tequila?" Sim grins and finally pulls her pants up over her bony butt.

"I think we should ask," Maarta says, with a firm look at me. "There must be a reason those rooms are closed." She raises her chin and stalks to the bathroom.

Sim narrows her eyes. "If we ask, there's more opportunity for them to say no."

"Either way, let's do our homework, first," I say. "I don't want to move into a room that has a radiation leak or something." My holo vibrates with a text from TC. He's waiting in the hall. "I gotta go. You two going to the party?"

She nods. "We'll be down in a bit. I have a couple errands to run first."

In the corridor, TC is a vision to behold. He sports a shiny gold shirt that's open half-way down his chest and black pants tucked into short, soft, Lether ship-boots. His dark hair looks like a newly cut lawn, short and straight, waving slightly as he moves. He grins, and a diamond flashes at me.

I laugh, gesturing to his face. "Is that new?"

"The tooth? No, you just didn't notice it before." He smirks then reaches up to his mouth. "Yeah, it's new." He holds up his palm, and a tiny, gold-set diamond glints in the overhead lights. "It snaps right on." He sticks his fingers in his mouth again, and grins, the diamond back in place. "They're all the rage at the Techno-Inst this year."

"Remember how you were saying the crew treat you like a child?" I ask. If he can't figure out what I'm implying, explaining won't help.

"Yeah, I know, but I think it's too late to change their minds anyway. May as well have some fun."

We stroll down the hall toward the ladder. There are float tubes in the crew sections of the ship, but for short drops, the very steep stairs are faster. TC swings in and slides down the handrails, backwards. I follow him down to the next deck, using the rungs.

Music pulses down the hall, pulling us like a beacon toward crew dining. The overhead lights are out, and lasers flash. Inside, a thick press of bodies gyrates to the music, some of them wildly out of rhythm. Feeling old, I pull the SuperDens Ear Guards Ollie gave me out of my pocket and shove them into my ears. TC grins and sends me a thumbs up emoji.

We dance our way into the room. I detour to the serving line, currently masquerading as a bar. Grabbing a couple glasses with tacky umbrellas sticking out the top, I start to hand one off to TC. Then I stop. "How old are you?" I shout.

He grins. "I'm twenty. Anyway, we're outside the Planetary Perimeter, so the drinking age is sixteen." He jerks a thumb toward his chest. "Hospitality major, remember? I know this stuff."

I shrug and hand him the drink. I have no doubt he would have doctored the official rosters if he was underage anyway. I can't believe he's only a few years younger than me. I feel ancient in comparison. "How do you know we're outside the perimeter?"

"I checked the schedule. We crossed at ten this morning. I like to know what legal jurisdiction I'm under at all times, just in case." He points. "You should see your face. That's a joke. I checked because a passenger asked me earlier today."

"Didn't that seem suspicious to you? I mean, who would need to know that if they weren't contemplating criminal activity?" I slurp at my straw. The sweet, fruity flavor fills my mouth. I swallow, and warmth blooms in my stomach. I gesture to TC with my drink. "These are pretty strong."

TC grins. "That's the way I like them. Again, kidding. You worry too much. How *old* are you?" He emphasizes the word 'old'.

I lift my chin. "I'm only twenty-four," I reply with dignity.

TC's grin widens. "Then let's party!"

A couple hours and several fruity drinks later, I'm slumped on a chair in the corner of the room. Across the way, Maarta is dancing with Ollie. The big man has some amazing moves on that glide chair of his. Sim came in a while ago, but I can't see her through the crowds. A man named Julian—part of the award-winning culinary team—talked my ear off about varieties of cheese but departed when a woman from propulsion asked him to dance. Now, TC sits across the table from me, his head down on the table. He talked big, but when it came down to connecting with people, he struck out.

I tap him on the shoulder. "You need to just be yourself," I shout.

He turns his head, raising his bleary eyes to mine without leaving the table. "Nobody wants the real me," he moans.

"Sure, they do. You just have to stop hiding him behind the arrogant *box*." I slurp the dregs of my last drink. "That guy is *carpet* annoying. Hey, they changed the swear dictionary!"

TC sits up. "Really? *Poster. Arm chair*. This is so *toilet* hysterical! How can the OS hear us over that music?"

I shrug. "Magic? You want another drink?"

"Nah, I think I'm going to turn in." TC lurches to his feet. "How late is it, anyway?"

I glance at my holo and stifle a laugh. "It's eleven thirty, grandpa."

TC turns red but smiles. "You got me. I'm not much of a party animal."

I stand up and gesture toward the door. "Yeah, me neither. Let's get out of here."

Outside, I pull the earplugs out and shove them back into my pocket. I will have to remember to thank Ollie for those. Now who sounds like a grandparent? My holo-ring vibrates the text signal.

"I gotta go," I tell TC.

His eyes flick from my face, to my palm, and back to my face. "Was that your station boyfriend?"

"You're too observant." I sigh. "Yeah, he and Ambar were done an hour ago, but I missed the text." I gaze absently through the door into the dining hall. The throngs have thinned, just a bit, and a space forms on the dance floor. A couple swings out, performing some kind of fast, jazzy number. The crowd cheers and catcalls.

"You aren't into all this dance stuff?" TC stands beside me, watching the action.

"Not really. I mean I like to dance, but I have no desire to compete. What about you?" A second couple whirls out onto the floor, and the first melts into the crowd.

"Two left feet," he says. "If I'd known dancing was expected here, I'd have requested a dirt-side internship."

"Hey!" I interrupt him. "That's Random and Kindra! Who's watching the store?"

CHAPTER TWELVE

TC GIVES ME A PUZZLED LOOK.

"They—" I point an accusing finger at the dancers "—are supposed to be on duty in Ops."

"Oooh, someone's in trouble! Are you gonna tell?"

I shake my head. "No, I'm not tattling. But I am not doing her work tomorrow." I flick into the OS and copy a few minutes of vid from the dining hall cams, making sure the date and time stamps are visible. "But I'm not above getting proof in case I need leverage, later."

We take the float tubes up. TC steps out on Deck F and waves as I continue upward. On N Deck, I make my way to the front of the ship. I knock on the door of the Maia Suite, but Ty doesn't answer. I pull up the ship schematic—he's back in the SolarDeck.

I'm too tired to go back to my crappy bunk right now, and I'm feeling kind of cheated since O'Neill isn't here. I use a back door to hack into the OS and unlock the door. The serene decor soothes my flustered nerves. Letting out a long sigh, I collapse on the sofa, pull a throw over myself and go to sleep.

The whoosh of the door opening drags me out of a confused dream about TC and my mother dancing in the zero grav gym on SK2. Kara and ancient Don Huatang tangoed nearby. This whole dance thing is really getting into my head.

A giggle pops my eyes open. In the open doorway, Ty stands with his back to me. I'd recognize him anywhere, even silhouetted against the light from the hallway. Behind him, a shadowed, but obviously female figure moves in close. She slides her hands over his shoulders and into his hair. "Aren't you going to invite me in, darling?"

Blood surges up into my face, rushing through my ears so loud I can't hear his response.

The woman presses herself against him, pushing him back a step into the room. He stumbles and grabs for the door frame. She shimmies against him and laughs, a deep, sexy laugh. "Come on, you know you want me."

I sit up. Neither of them notices me. But I notice his arm around the woman's waist. "Agent O'Neill," I snap. Their heads whip around. "Send your little plaything on her way and shut the door," I flick on the light over the doorway.

Lady Grandelle squeals and takes a half step back. She looks furious. "You didn't tell me you had someone waiting for you! I don't share." She spins on her heel and stalks away.

O'Neill shuts the door and turns to face me. "Thank God you were here. I wasn't sure how I was going to get rid of her."

"Right." My voice is still hard. "You brought the Grendel to your cabin because you wanted to get rid of her."

He laughs then blinks as if surprised. "She followed me here. I didn't invite her! Why would I?" He drops onto the couch and slides over next to me. "I have you."

I try to stay angry, but he's just so sincere. "Do you? Have me?"

"Don't I?" He leans away to look at my face. "Am I really in trouble over the Grendel? Check the vids—I didn't encourage her at all! She's like a Starvorian Sand Dragon: a cold, scaly, predator." He shudders dramatically.

I relax against him. "I believe you. I'm not sure why. Probably because you compared your girlfriend to a lizard."

"Not my girlfriend!" He slides an arm around me. "That would be you, and you're nothing like a lizard."

I smile. That's what I wanted to hear. And I can always check the vid feeds later.

THE NEXT MORNING, I swing in to Ops a few minutes early. Kindra's smile is brittle. Random mutters under his breath and ignores me. They both look hungover. Or maybe they're still drunk. Before I came in this morning, I checked the Ops vids, and they came back to work only about ninety minutes ago.

"That was some party, last night," I say in a flat voice. "Too bad you missed it."

Kindra logs out of her station and rolls her eyes at me. "Yeah, too bad. What game are you playing?"

"Me?" I stare into her eyes. Her lids flicker and she looks away. "I'm just doing my job. I appreciate others who do the same."

"What's that supposed to mean?" Kindra advances across the room toward me. "I get my job done. I do it well! I don't need some new *curtain rod* making trouble for me!"

The door slides open. Ollie takes one look at our faces and eases back out. Coward.

"I'm not making trouble," I reply evenly. "But I'm not cleaning up after anyone too 'busy' to finish their work."

The other woman narrows her eyes at me. "If you—"

Random sweeps between us, sliding an arm around Kindra and turning her toward the door. "Nice to see you Triana," Random says. "Have a good shift."

Before I can respond, they're gone, and Ollie glides in. I shake my head at him. "Thanks for the help."

Ollie lifts his shoulders, hands warding me off. "Stay cool."

"I'll stay cool if the dashboard is green." I log in to my console and pull up the maintenance dash. Once I've swiped all Kindra's complete-but-not-cleared tickets into the corral I built yesterday, there are surprisingly few flashing items. Most of them were reported early this morning, but a few less vital problems remain from last night. "We'd have a lot less work to do if they did theirs," I grumble.

Ollie shrugs again. "Gives us something to do."

"That's a pretty generous attitude." I get to work.

A MELODIOUS CHIME rings through the room and my audio implant. "Attention, passengers and crew. This is Captain Santiago el-Hadri Swanson Olimar ne Bundoir. As you know, we're scheduled to jump to the Sally Ride system this morning. We are approaching our jump belt on schedule. Jump will commence in thirty minutes. Passengers, please make your way to the nearest jump lounge. Crew, run your checks and report your stations."

Ollie stretches his arms and shoulders, looking over at me. "You know how to report?"

"I read the manual." I swipe through a couple screens and log my location into the OS. Hyper-jumps are common and relatively safe but ships still follow procedures. Early jumps occasionally resulted in someone disappearing during the transit. Current technology prevents that issue, for the most part, but the tradition of checking all passengers and crew both before and after a jump remains.

Out of curiosity, I pull up the passenger logs, and find O'Neill. He's in the Eurypylus Lounge. I pull up vids from the room and zoom in on his table. He's sitting at a four-top with two other passengers and Ambar. I grit my teeth. Taking a deep breath, I sigh it out, long and slow. If I'd known this trip was going to arouse so much jealousy in me, I would have refused the job.

"You seen Les?" Ollie's voice makes me jump.

"Not today." I swipe a few screens. "She hasn't reported in yet, but maybe she needs to be in a particular location?"

Ollie shakes his head. "This is her duty station. She should be here. She's not showing on the locator."

"What do you mean she's not showing? Everyone shows on the locator!" The OS tracks every crew member's location at all times. It's one of the reasons I worried about spending time in O'Neill's suite. But after Random and Kindra's blatant performance last night, I stopped worrying about it. If they can wander during their shift, I'll do what I want off-duty.

Ollie cracks his knuckles. "She's not on the locator."

I scroll through the lists. I pull her ID number from the employment records and search on that. I check the stats on her cabin. "She hasn't logged anywhere since yesterday about ten. How is that possible? Maybe she's drunk and sleeping it off?"

"Since ten yesterday morning? Not like her." Ollie scrubs his hands over his dark, shiny scalp. "Besides, she wouldn't take off her ring."

"Could it be a glitch?"

"The OS tracks every ring on the ship, even the unregistered ones. Even glitchy ones." He flicks through a few screens. "Not finding any dead rings, either."

Massaging my temples, I think aloud. "As I see it, there are two possibilities. Either she went AWOL or someone did something to her. If she chose to hide, how and why would she do that? And if she's not hiding, then are we talking about a crime?"

Ollie's big hands swipe through screens at incredible speed. "I'm matching guests to unregistered rings, and they all belong to passengers. Check the vids." He flings a file to me.

I pop open the file and find a list of unregistered rings and their current locations. With a flick, I search and find cams in each location. Vid feeds give me access to virtually the entire ship. I pull up a vid link to each location, one after the next. No Les, no Les, no Les. "So, if she is on the ship, she's not wearing an active ring," I say slowly.

"Where else would she be?" He spins his chair toward me.

"Can you access the external hatch logs?" My stomach curdles at the thought. If she was thrown off the ship, we'd never find her body. The perfect murder.

His hands a blur, Ollie scrambles through the system.

I hold my breath.

"No hatch pops." He lets out a sigh. "She has to be on board."

I collapse back in my seat. "Do we need to call security?"

Ollie snorts. "Security here is a joke. They'll look at the log we just checked and call it absent without leave. Since her ring isn't registering, it must be in a shielded location. Or flushed."

A hard laugh escapes from my mouth. Plumbing systems are one of the few ways to truly hide a holo-ring on a ship or station. "It'll show up in a few days, then. Unless—" I pinch the bridge of my nose. "Does this ship vent anything?"

Ollie shakes his head. "We're green. Everything is recycled."

"So, it's possible she flushed or shielded her ring and is hiding somewhere on board. Why would she do that?"

He shrugs. "Wants to quit?"

"Does she?" I ask. "She seemed pretty happy with the status quo."

Ollie's lips twitch. "Dunno. We aren't that close."

The chimes sound again. "Jump will commence in five minutes. Please engage security. Initiating pre-jump checklist. Ops?"

Ollie and I flip switches, engaging the security fields that will hold us in place during jump. We flick through the screens, looking for the flashing red that would indicate a restraint failure or loose passenger. Crew are trained to secure children first, so hopefully there are no wandering toddlers.

"All secure." Ollie flicks his green-go icon.

"Ops reports all secure," the first officer's voice echoes through the room. "Maintenance?"

"All secure," I repeat, flicking my own green.

"Maintenance reports all secure," the first officer drones on. "Propulsion?"

I turn down the volume, relying on the screens to notify us if anything goes wrong. Hyper jump is so routine these days that running through these protocols feels archaic. "Well, there's nothing we can do about Les right now." I wave a hand at the pre-jump checklist changing from red to green as we watch.

Ollie nods. "We'll look for her after jump."

Everyone experiences jump a little differently. For me, it feels like a wave washing through the ship. I can almost hear it coming toward me, then it washes through me and away. I've heard other people describe it as their cells being flipped upside down, or a fizzle through their veins, or a flash of cold or heat. Some people are so traumatized the first time that they never travel again, but it's kind of a non-issue for me. Probably because my Mother took me on my first long-distance voyage when I was still in diapers.

Ollie shakes all over like a dog and deactivates his security field. He slides back out of his desk. "Let's go."

I stare at him. "Where are we going? Someone has to stay here."

"I forwarded the calls." He waves his holo-ring at me. "Besides, Les is the only one who would check on us, and she's missing."

"If we can just forward the calls, why do we stay in here all day?" I flip my incoming reports feed to my holo-ring.

Ollie shrugs and glides out the door. "Rules."

Waving the door shut, I run after him. "But where are we going to look? She could be anywhere?"

"Dunno, but I gotta look."

"Ollie," I call. He spins around, staring at me. "I'm going to backtrack through the vids and see where she disappeared."

He gives me a thumbs up. "Send me the info."

Shaking my head, I walk back into the Ops room. Maybe he just needs to get out of this closet for a while, but where can he possibly look that we can't check via vid? I pull up the stored videos starting with our departure from SK2. Cross-referencing them with the location report from Les' holo-ring should bring me to her last reported location.

Which was here, yesterday morning. She walked out that door and disappeared from the system. How is that even possible? I look for backup logs. First backup after her departure was yesterday at noon. No record of her after she left the room. Zark.

I call Ollie. "Where are you?"

"Gym. She comes here a lot." Ollie flips on his visual, and I can see work out machines and free weights, currently racked and locked for jump. Ollie grunts.

"Are you working out, Ollie?" Does no one actually work a full day here? He doesn't answer. "Look, Les disappeared from the system when she left Ops yesterday. I'm going to run some facial recognition software on the vid feeds. I'll let you know what I find." He grunts again, so I sign off.

I feed the ship's video through a special program I brought with me from SK2. Then I turn my attention to clearing maintenance tickets.

About an hour later, I get a ping. The app found three frames of video with part of Les's face on them after she disappeared from here. There's a pic of the back of her head in the purser's office, a side shot in a hallway, and a distant shot of her down on Alpha deck, near propulsion. Someone must have gone through all the vid and deleted her. Current software makes that pretty easy, but it still requires time and access.

I pull the logs, but almost half the ship's staff has access. If I could get into the HR records, I could see who likely has the skill, but HR is more carefully protected than security. Screwed up system, if you ask me.

Flicking open the comms program, I call O'Neill. I watch his icon on the ship schematic as he leaves the Eurypylus Lounge and steps out into a corridor.

"Hey, beautiful, what's up?" His face pops up on my screen. He's smiling and his voice is cheerful.

"Beautiful?" I wrinkle my nose. "That's new."

"I heard one of the bartenders call a passenger that, and she seemed to like it." He shrugs. "I thought I'd try it out. You don't like it?"

"I can't complain about being called beautiful, I guess." I narrow my eyes. "But you know those guys use nicknames like that, so they don't have to remember people's real names."

He holds up a hand. "I won't call anyone else beautiful, I promise!"

"Fair enough, *stud*." I pinch my lips together to hide my grin. It fades when I remember why I'm calling. "Much as I enjoy flirting with you, I need to talk to *Agent* O'Neill, now."

His face changes, hardening a little. "What's the problem?"

"Can I meet you in the dance studio?"

He blinks, but nods. "Sure. Now?"

"Yes, please. I'll see you in about five, okay?" Without waiting for a reply, I terminate the call and ping Ollie. "I'm leaving Ops, can you cover the calls?"

"On my way," Ollie confirms, and the connection goes dark.

As I log out of the system and shut down my station, the door slides open. Ollie glides in and scoots to his place without a word. He must have been on his way back when I called.

"I found three frames of video with Les's face." I flick the pics to him. "Someone deleted her from the vid files. Who could do that?'

Ollie stares at me for a beat, then his eyes unfocus. "You. Me. Kindra. Random. Timmons, Sandel, Arriaen. Lots more." He focuses on me again. "You want a list?"

"Yeah, if you don't mind. As much info as you can give me on each of them. I haven't hacked into the HR. Yet." I grin.

Ollie grins back. "I'm on it."

"My friend is a security agent from SK2." I pause by the door. "I'm going to see if he has any suggestions. I'll be back soon."

"Take your time. I know where to find you." He gestures to a ship schematic with my icon blinking.

"As long as I don't disappear like Les. Keep an eye on me, will you?" I wave and take off down the hall.

CHAPTER THIRTEEN

INSIDE THE DANCE STUDIO, I pace back and forth in front of the programmable window. I've set it to transparent, just to be sure no one is watching from over there. I've also paused the cams on this room and disabled the microphones. After a few seconds consideration, I activate one of the cams, and send the vid to a hidden memory location so I can access it later. Just in case.

As I finish up the coding and swiping, the door slides open. O'Neill strides in, followed by Ambar and the dance instructor. O'Neill shrugs and makes a face.

"This is Triana Moore," he tells the two women, gesturing to me. "Triana, this is Joan, and I think you've met Ambar?"

Ambar narrows her eyes at me. Then, noticing Ty watching her, she smiles. "Yes, we embarked together. So good to see you again, *Technician* Moore." She puts a tiny emphasis on the title, as if to put me in my place.

"Hi, Ambar. Guess you must have finally gotten that centerpiece finished?" While she glowers, I turn to the other woman and bump fists. "Nice to meet you, Joan. Are you rehearsing today? I thought you did evenings?"

Joan smiles and opens her mouth, but Ambar interrupts. "I got off early to practice. We have some minor details to tweak." She sits down on the floor to change into her dance shoes.

Joan lets out a silent sigh. "Perfect practice makes perfect. Do you dance, Triana?"

"Me? I'm not joining your crazy competition!" I ward her off with my hands. "No dancing. No singing. No performing. At all."

Ty laughs. "I think you got your point across, T."

T? I give him a quizzical look, then turn back to Joan. "Can I borrow him for a moment? Just some ah, station matters to discuss."

Ambar's head pops up. "Station matters? We aren't on the station. It will have to wait! We must rehearse!"

Joan winks and turns to Ambar. "You and I are going to work on your spins first anyway. Ty can do his warm up after he and Triana are done talking."

I don't wait for Ambar to argue. I just grab O'Neill's arm and hustle him out of the room.

"Sorry about that," he says as the door swishes shut behind us. "I tried to give her the slip, but she followed me out of the Lounge. Then we ran into Joan down here."

I wave him off and walk a few paces down the hall. "Doesn't matter. Listen, I need your investigative expertise. Les is missing."

"Who's Les?" He leans against the wall.

"She's my boss." I think for a minute. "Well, kind of. She's the Ops supervisor. I don't technically report to her— It doesn't matter. Ollie and I saw her yesterday morning around ten and she hasn't shown up anywhere on the ship, since." I explain about the holo-ring not responding and the three frames of video.

"Any hatch pops?"

My nose twitches. "That's what I asked, but no, we didn't find any. And the ship is green—no dumps at all."

"So, she has to be on board. Did you call Security?" He drums his fingers against the wall.

"I suggested that, but Ollie says they're worthless."

"If you can't find her, you need to report it. Even if they're worthless.

Gotta have it on the record." He runs his fingers through his hair. As always, it falls back into perfect style.

I smile a little whenever he does that. It reminds me of the first time I saw him—the shiniest guy I'd ever met. "Yeah, we'll do that. But I thought you might have some ideas of how to investigate."

He shrugs. "If you can't follow her ring or vid trail, then someone went to a great deal of effort to hide her. Could she be going AWOL?"

I thrust my fingers into my own hair, knowing it will result in a rat's nest. "Don't know. I guess we should see if we can figure out who her friends were on the ship?"

"Sounds like a good place to start," he says. "I'll try to get away from here as soon as I can."

Behind me, the door slides open and Ambar's voice quavers through the passageway "Ty! I need you!"

O'Neill's eyes almost roll. He glances over my shoulder, then straightens up from the wall. Snaking an arm around my waist, he pulls me close and kisses me, fast and hard. Holding me close, he spins us down the hall. His body and arms are warm and solid, but gentle. The spin is effortless and graceful, almost like flying. I feel as if we could whirl the full length of the ship and back to SK2. This man can dance! If this is what dancing with Ty feels like, maybe I should change my mind about the competition.

"Gotta go." He gives a little nudge at my waist and holds up my hand. I spin away and stop by the door. Magic.

As he disappears into the room, Ambar shoots me a furious look from the doorway. I smile and give her a little finger wave, then head back to Ops with a warm feeling in my belly.

THE REST of the afternoon passes slowly. Ollie has no idea who Les hangs out with when she's off duty. Like everyone else on this boat, she went to the gym, a lot. And, of course, she ate some meals in the crew mess. But no one Ollie has asked knows what she did the rest of her time off.

Between maintenance tickets, I prowl through the video feeds from the previous leg of the cruise. And, occasionally, I peek into the live feed from Studio I-14. Maybe more than occasionally.

Joan takes them through a sequence of steps, about eight bars of music, over and over. They do it so many times, I have it memorized. I could probably dance it in my sleep.

Ty is really good. Ambar is almost as bad as he is good. Her sense of rhythm is practically non-existent, and she has two left feet. At the end of the sequence, there's a drop, where Ty holds her hands, and she drops to the floor, stopping parallel with the deck, just a few centimeters above it. At least, that's what's supposed to happen. Joan takes Ambar's place and demonstrates the move. Spin. Down. Up!

"I know how to do it!" Ambar whines, pushing Joan out of the way. She steps into Ty's arms, and I grit my teeth. He spins her out, and then in. She trips over her feet and plows right into him. Ty staggers. I giggle.

"Again!" Joan says. "Five, six, seven, eight!"

Ty spins her out again and back in. This time she makes the turn but misses his hand.

"When you spin in, put your hand up like this." Joan holds her free hand at chest height. She and Ty do the move, slowly. "If you put your hand here, it will meet his, and you'll get a good grip on his wrist. Then you're ready for the drop."

Ambar kind of growls and takes her place again. This time, she gets her hand up too high and smacks Ty in the face.

"Ow!" He rubs his cheek.

"Try again." Joan paces around the edges of the dance floor, watching, her blue eyes missing nothing.

Ty spins Ambar out and in. She gets her hand up and grips his wrist. But instead of dropping gracefully, slowed by Ty's hold, Ambar flings herself toward the ground. The force yanks Ty off balance and he crashes on top of her.

Ambar bursts into tears.

Ollie barks out a laugh. He's watching the same vid feed. He glances at me. "She's funny."

"Did you hook into the cam in Studio I-14?"

Ollie shakes his head and flicks the feed to my console. Although it's the same view I'm watching, there's a banner across the top that reads "Dancing in the Stars!" And a small blinking green box with the word LIVE! in the bottom corner.

"They're broadcasting the dance rehearsal?" I sputter.

Ollie nods. "Always do. Especially the funny ones."

I lean my head back against my chair and groan. "Do they know?" I wave at the screen.

Ollie shrugs. "It's in the contract."

Of course, it is. I wonder if O'Neill read his.

I go back to the files from the previous leg from Grissom to Kaku. Using my superior hacking skills, I set up a loop to pull every clip of Les. I can follow her from the moment she leaves her cabin, through her whole day, and into her off duty hours. Except when she's in private spaces, like a stateroom.

Actually, I discover she's visible in her cabin as well. The Pleiades Line is breaking some pretty serious privacy laws. I find files of every cabin, passenger and crew, around the clock.

I search for the video from cabin C-251 from this leg and see myself changing clothes this morning. "Forking *footstools!* Those *window shades!*"

"Did you find the illegal vids?" Ollie peeks at my screens.

I round on him. "You knew? And you didn't warn me?"

Ollie cowers back a fraction, holding up his hands. "You're pretty smart. I figured you'd check."

I rub my temple. "I should have. What else did I miss?"

Ollie shrugs. "That's all I know."

I go back to the vids and get an eyeful of Sim in her favorite condition—she does nude yoga in the middle of the day. Yeesh. I cut the feed from my cabin. I'm about to send a virus to the cam software but think better of it. I divert the signal to the hidden memory pocket I've spliced into OS storage. Add a passphrase set, and no one can access it but me. Just in case I need a record of anything that happens in there. I work on O'Neill's suite next. Then I divert the feeds from all the active staff cabins, too, just for good measure.

Back to Les. Modifying my facial recognition software, I set the system to track her movements and give me a condensed version. By the time the program is set, my shift is over. Kindra and Random arrive twenty minutes late. I grind my teeth and follow Ollie out into the hall.

"Is this how it goes? They show up later and later each day?" I ask.

Ollie shrugs. "Only till we make station. They're on time at the beginning of each leg."

"And you're okay with that? We won't reach Crippen-Hauck for two more days." I follow him down the hall without thinking.

He shrugs again. "Just come in late in the morning. It all evens out. You coming to the gym?" He glides to a halt by the float tube.

"That'd be a big no," I say with a dry laugh. "I'm going to see if O'Neill can help us with Les. He thinks we should report it to security."

"Already did." Ollie turns and glides into the float tube. "They said *thanks*." And he zips out of sight.

Thanks. What kind of security agent says 'thanks' when you tell them a woman is missing? One who doesn't care.

Or one who already knows she's missing?

CHAPTER FOURTEEN

ACCORDING to my slightly illegal tracking app, O'Neill is still in Studio I-14. The live Dancing in the Stars feed has moved on to a different couple, but my tap into the studio cam is live. Ambar and Joan practice a fancy step at a very slow speed. O'Neill sits on a chair in the corner, holding something to his face. His body is slumped, and he looks exhausted.

I close the app and hurry up to I Deck. The door to Studio I-14 is open, and I can hear Ambar crying from ten doors down. For the briefest moment, I consider turning tail and running, but I don't want to leave O'Neill in there with the incredible bawling woman.

"Hi." I lean through the doorway. O'Neill's eyes light up when he sees me. At least, the one I can see lights up. The other is covered by an ice-pac. "What happened to you?"

"You!" Ambar pulls her arm out of Joan's grip and stalks across the floor. She glares at me from puffy, bloodshot eyes. Tear streaks stain her face, and her skin is blotchy. "You totally threw me off my game! You need to stay away from us—I can't focus on my dancing when I know you're there, smirking!"

I stare at her. "What? Where?"

She waves her hands vaguely around the room. "Here! There! Anywhere!

I can't deal with all the judgement!" The tears start to pour down her face again. She should get points for sheer volume. It's amazing she's not dehydrated. With a growl, she stomps out of the room.

I raise my eyebrows at Joan. She shrugs and opens her mouth. Holding up a finger to silence her, I face the cam hidden in the corner of the room. "Rehearsal is over. Under the terms of our contracts, we revoke live vid coverage."

A heavy sigh whooshes out of the corner speaker. "Come on, Technician! This is gold!"

"Nope, we're done here. Cams off till tomorrow's rehearsal." I cross my arms. "And I know how to check, so no funny business." I turn to Joan and Ty. "Tell them you revoke coverage."

Joan grins. "I revoke coverage until I go back on duty tomorrow."

"I, uh, revoke coverage," Ty fumbles, "until tomorrow's rehearsal?" He looks at me for confirmation.

I nod. "Yup, that's it, we're all out. Cams off." I pull up my OS connection and check the vid feeds. "You're still recording."

"We always record the public spaces, Technician," the voice says with a hint of a whine. "But we cut distribution."

"Yeah, I should trust you why?" Using the code slip TC gave me, I scramble the cam feed.

"Hey!"

"What the *valance*?"

Joan turns off the speaker.

"They're filming us?" Ty asks, his voice choked.

Joan and I nod. "Didn't you read the contract?" we ask, almost in unison.

"Contract?" he asks.

"It's part of your ticket purchase agreement. Participating in the dance competition constitutes approval to record all competition-related activities and use said recording in promotional materials. Or something like that." Joan shrugs. "No one reads the fine print."

"Doesn't matter," I say while Ty's jaw hinges open and closed a couple times. "They're recording everything on board anyway. Legal or not."

Joan's eyes narrow. "Everything?"

"Yup," I pop the p on the end of the word. "I already cut the feeds from all the crew cabins." Ignoring her angry exclamation, I turn to O'Neill, gesturing to his face. "What happened?"

He pulls the ice-pac away and reveals a magnificent black eye. "Ambar tried a kick without looking for obstructions. I'm lucky I don't have a bloody nose or broken jaw."

I whistle, impressed. "A kick to the head, hard enough to give you a black eye? I didn't think she had that kind of range or flexibility! That's *Vanti* impressive." Vanti is O'Neill's practically perfect former partner. She's annoyingly amazing.

Joan barks out a laugh. "Yeah, no. She's not that flexible or accurate. Ty was bending over to tie his shoe. That's why the vid producer was so ticked when you shut him down. He was hoping you'd pitch a fit and start a cat fight when you discovered what happened."

'Ugh!" I groan. "Maybe we should get you to a med-pod before it swells completely shut."

"There's one in the spa. I can get us in," Joan says. We step out into the hall, and she closes up the studio behind us.

"Why didn't you go there right away?" I slide an arm around Ty's waist.

"It just happened a few minutes ago." He pulls me in close. "She was so distraught, I didn't want to leave Joan alone with her. She's almost unhinged sometimes."

Behind us, Joan laughs. "Dancing does that to some people. I've seen couples who are madly in love turn into raging lunatics when their partner can't get a move right. It's both frightening and hilarious. And one of the reasons I'm single!"

We reach the end of the wide hall and turn into a narrow cross corridor. A passing couple give O'Neill a strange look. A few meters along, Joan waves open an unmarked door. "Employee entrance."

Lights spring on illuminating a utilitarian break room. Cupboards and counters line the walls. A pair of AutoKich'ns take up one counter. Worn plastek chairs sit empty by a scarred table. I catch a faint whiff of sandalwood and eucalyptus incense. Joan leads the way across the room to another door and waves it open.

We step into another world. The fragrance intensifies. Lush green plants grow in huge planters, somehow looking natural yet tidy. An enormous, golden statue dominates the room. From this angle, it looks like a chubby, bald guy in a diaper sitting on a box. A waterfall rumbles to life as we walk past.

"Motion activated," Joan says. "The spa is available around the clock. You have to make an appointment, of course, but the massage therapists refuse to learn how to work the technology. So, it's as automated as possible. Come on, the med-pod is in here."

She leads us past open doors that lead to individual therapy rooms. We cross the misty foyer by the waterfall, and skirt around the golden statue smiling down at us. A recording of exotic bird calls and gently chiming music adds to the ambiance.

At the front, behind a neat screen of frondy green plants, we find a door marked with the first aid blue star. Joan waves it open, and we step inside. A state-of-the-art med-pod sits against the wall. I pop the seal, and O'Neill lies down inside.

Before closing the lid, I give him a kiss. "Haven't we done this before?"

He grins, then winces. "That was much worse. This is pretty minor. It should only take a few minutes." The translucent lid settles down over him, and the scan begins.

A calm, androgynous voice announces: "Diagnosis: minor ecchymosis. Estimated time to complete treatment: four minutes."

Joan sits down on a rolling stool. "How'd a maintenance tech end up with a guy like that?"

I laugh, hoisting myself up onto a counter. "That's a long story. He needed some help on a case, and I have access to pretty much everywhere on the station."

Joan grins. "I'll bet you do."

I shrug. "How'd you end up on this cruise?"

"That's an equally long story," she replies. "I learned to dance as a kid. After twenty years in the Marines, I retired and went back to my roots. I like to travel, so this is a great way to make a little credit. This is my first time with Pleiades, but I've worked on most of the big cruise lines."

I stare at her in amazement. "You were a Marine?"

"*Semper Fi.*" She flips me a casual salute. "Once a Marine, always a Marine."

"You packing?"

Joan looks uncomfortable. "I do dirtside, but cruise ships have a strict no weapons policy. It took me a while to get comfortable with that, I can tell you! But even unarmed, I can take care of myself."

She looks so competent lounging there, I believe her. "What did you do, all those years in the Marines?"

"What didn't I do?" Joan grins again. "I started out in infantry, then did some sniping, some search and rescue. Then I moved into maintenance and ended up in cryptography. I've been all over the galactic sector."

"That seems like a strange combination of jobs."

"It is," she admits. "I get bored if I don't get to learn new stuff, so I moved around a bit. It meant I made rank more slowly, but I can do just about anything." She cracks her knuckles.

The lid of the med-pod pops and lifts slowly. O'Neill sits up, his face back to its usual, perfect appearance. He smiles. "Good as new!"

Joan leaps to her feet. "You two got plans for the evening? With Ambar out of the way, I have a free night. Wanna go dancing?"

O'Neill's jaw drops. "More dancing?"

"Yeah, but just for fun." Joan leads the way out of the room. "There's a great club down on H Deck. We could grab some dinner, then get our cha-cha on!" She does a little dance step past the giant, gold dude. She gives me a considering look. "We'll get you up to speed in no time, Triana. You move like a dancer."

I hold up a hand. "I dunno. Your overzealous cam crew might decide dancing constitutes a dance-comp-related activity and put us back on the live show."

"Who cares? It'll be so much more fun without the amazing weeping woman. I've never met a person with less rhythm than Ambar." Joan waves open the door, and we step out into the hall.

"I can't believe you want to dance more." O'Neill rubs his jaw.

Joan laughs. "I don't get to really dance when I'm teaching. Plus, it's not as painful when your partner has some talent. Or training."

"Let's get some dinner," I say. "We can talk about dancing later."

"Deal." Joan takes us to her favorite diner on G Deck, the lowest deck open to passengers. They serve standard diner fare, like Tafo and Dumplings, and Ruggarian Noodles. The place is relatively empty, so the three of us easily find a booth.

"How does that whole, 'you must be in uniform' thing work for you?" I ask Joan.

"I'm a contractor, so the usual rules don't apply to me. Plus, this is my uniform." She gestures at her stretchy leggings and long tunic top.

O'Neill glances at Joan and raises an eyebrow at me. "Did you find any additional info about your, uh, boss?"

I consider Joan. I took a quick peek at her personnel file while she was in the bathroom. She's been on the ship since Grissom. Before that, she worked as a show choreographer for Orion Cruises, and as a dancer on a touring company of *Fantôme de la Cirque*, the huge musical production about a crazy guy who lives under a circus.

But her background in the Marines could come in handy if there's any funny business going on. Plus, the fact that she's fairly new to the ship means she probably isn't involved in the illegal recording. Of course, she could have killed Les and fed her into the bio-recycler, but I haven't seen any indication of insanity or a connection to Les or anyone else on the ship. And, I trust her. For some reason.

I shrug. "We can't find any trace of her. I set a loop running to track her movements on the previous leg, since she was deleted from this one. There's no indication she left the ship at SK2, so whatever is going on is probably tied to the ship, not our current location. But who knows? Maybe she just keeled over dead somewhere."

"That doesn't explain why her ring stopped transmitting." O'Neill replies absently, while perusing the menu on the table screen. "How's the Manchurian Fry?"

Joan blinks. "It's good. A little spicy, but not burn-your-mouth hot. And I'm a wimp when it comes to food. What's all this talk about being dead?"

I stab the table to enter my order and look up. "Les Santiago is missing. Do you know her?"

"Missing? How can someone go missing on a cruise ship? They track everyone." Joan enters her own order. After a minute, she shakes her head. "Can't say I've met her. But I mostly interact with the passengers and the crew who are dancing. She wasn't on the roster. There's a guy at the gym who knows everyone. You should ask him. I can introduce you."

"Why is everyone on this ship obsessed with the gym?" I grump.

"It's a small ship." Joan shrugs. "There are only so many places to go. If you live in a can this size for very long, you have to figure out some way to get some exercise. Besides, Marine, remember? We like to stay fit." She makes a fist, flexing her bicep. "But Ollie knows everyone."

"Ollie? Big, dark-skinned dude with a bald head and full beard?" I ask. At her nod, I continue. "He and I work together. He's the one who noticed she's missing."

She slaps her forehead. "Of course. Ops. Maintenance. I knew that. Besides, Ollie knows everyone." A wait-bot trundles up, and she pulls out drinks for all of us.

"Did you have any luck tracking down any other friends?" O'Neill takes a sip of his beer.

"She didn't have any." I make condensation circles on the plas table with my glass. "At least, not that we've found. You'd think one of them would have reported her missing. Maybe they did! Maybe that's why Security was so blasé—because they already got a report?" I turn to O'Neill. "Can you offer to help and see if they'll tell you anything?"

He raises an eyebrow. "It's worth a try. But, if they're already investigating, surely, they'd have interrogated you and Ollie. You were the last ones to see her, and you're her co-workers."

"I've got a loop tracking her movements from the Grissom-Kaku run. Maybe we can find some friends from that." I reach over and pick up a red bottle. "What's this?"

"*Kech-on*," Joan replies. "Supposedly some Ancient Earth condiment made from tomatoes."

"Huh." I set the bottle back down. "I've heard of that. But I think it's *kachip*, not *kech-on*. I watch a lot of *Ancient TēVē*."

"A lot," O'Neill confirms.

As the food arrives, my holo-ring pings. "Ooh, this is the loop I was telling you about!" I pull up the results. "Here's the report, starting when the ship departed Grissom. She left Ops at 6:30 pm. Went to dinner, sat alone. Went to the gym. Went to cabin D-47. Next day, left cabin D-47, went to work. Went to dinner. Went to the gym. Went home. This is the most boring person I've ever stalked."

"Stalked a lot of folks, have you?" Joan pokes her fork into her cheesy noodle dish and steam wafts out. "I haven't done that much stalking myself, but that sounds about like my dad's schedule. Except he works a ranch instead of a cruise ship."

I roll my eyes and pick up a dumpling with my chopsticks. Half-way into my mouth, the temperature registers. "Hot! Hot! Hot!" Dropping the dumpling, I gulp down half my beer.

O'Neill snickers. "It just came out of the oven-bot—what did you expect?"

I ignore him, scrolling down the report further. "Hey, on the third day out, she went to cabin B-186 instead of D-47."

"Hot date?" O'Neill suggests.

I flick the link and pull up the holo on my palm. "There's no one with her, so if it's a hot date, she met him/her/them, there."

"I don't suppose you can pull up a record of her holo-calls?" Joan asks. "So, we can see who she's meeting?"

I narrow my eyes at Joan. "That's a pretty good suggestion for a beginner. Didn't you just say you've never stalked anyone before?"

"I think she said she's only stalked her dad." O'Neill points his loaded fork at her. "That's kind of sad. And creepy."

"I said Les's schedule sounds like my Dad's," Joan retorts. "I didn't say I stalked him. And what's sad about not having stalked anyone?"

O'Neill laughs. "I meant stalking your Dad is sad. Never mind." He pops the fork into his mouth. "This is tasty. Perfect heat level."

I hold up a finger. "While you two were he-said-she-said-ing, I've been working. I fast forwarded through the vid feed in passageway outside cabin B-186. Nobody ever goes in; nobody ever goes out. And I mean, no one. Except Les. Hang on." I flick a few more links then nod. "That's one of the cabins that's 'closed' for maintenance. This whole section is closed." I make air quotes to emphasize my skepticism.

Joan leans in. "There's a whole passageway of crew cabins closed for maintenance? Is that why I'm sharing with five other people? I almost jumped ship when they told me that. Never had to share with more than one before."

"I know! I've got five roommates, too. And this whole section is practically empty." I flip up a schematic and show her the color-coded rooms. B-186 is right in the middle. "Maybe Les was escaping her roommates?"

"I think we need to see what she was looking at. Can you pull up vid from that cabin? You said the cruise line is illegally watching all the crew cabins?" O'Neill scrapes some sauce off his plate with the edge of his fork. "That was excellent."

I look at his plate, then down at mine. "You're done already? Mine's still too hot to eat!"

He shrugs. "Time for dessert!"

"Good thing you have the high-metabolism mod," I say.

"They make those?" Joan asks.

"No. I wish. He's just lucky. He runs hot." I take a bite of my now cool dumpling. It *is* good.

Ty gives me a suggestive look. "Yeah, I do."

My cheeks heat, but fortunately, my coloring hides blushes pretty well.

Joan laughs. "You should see your face!"

Or maybe not.

I clear my throat. "Anyway. After we finish, let's go check out that cabin. I can get us in."

"Of course you can." O'Neill smiles. "And this isn't my ship, so I don't even need to pretend to protest."

"Well, technically, it belongs to your company." I can't resist.

"Do you want my help or not?" He sticks his fingers in his ears and raises his eyebrows. "La la la, la la. So, can you see what's inside that cabin?"

I shake my head. "There aren't any vids from the closed cabins. Which is pretty suspicious, if you ask me."

The bot arrives with O'Neill's dessert. Luckily for him, it's lemon cake, which is not my favorite. Of course, he knows that. I glare at him. "Lemon? Why lemon?"

"Because I wanted to eat it, and not just get a taste of the leftover crumbs." He smiles sweetly. "Don't worry, there's a chocolate lava cake coming when you're done with that."

This guy is a keeper.

CHAPTER FIFTEEN

I FINISH off the lava cake before O'Neil takes his last bite of lemon. I hate to scarf down something so good so quickly, but we have work to do. Plus, I can't resist chocolate. Joan just sips on a black coffee while we eat. No wonder she's so skinny.

We take a float tube down to B Deck and head across the ship to the far bulkhead. These are crew quarters, but on the opposite end and side from mine.

"Wow, these are really crammed in tight, aren't they?" O'Neill asks as we walk past door after door.

"Welcome to the servants' quarters. Where's your berth, Joan?"

"I'm up on D Deck. Guess they don't want the contractors mixing with the hired help, either."

"I thought you said you have five roommates?" O'Neill asks.

"I do." Joan does a funky little side-step. "This is a dance cruise, remember? There are at least a dozen dance instructors on this tub. Most of us are coaching, but a few are working with the entertainers. They're also contractors."

"Huh." I stop in front of a door. "I didn't realize there were so many irregular crew. Contractors, interns, temps. This is the one." I pop open my link to the OS and start looking for the door release.

It isn't where I expect. "These doors are all isolated from the regular system. I guess they don't want anyone wandering in. If there were some kind of life-threatening problem, that would make sense."

"But what could be life-threatening in the middle of the ship?" O'Neill asks. "These are internal cabins, right? Isn't there another passageway beyond them?

"Yeah, two, in fact," I mutter, flicking and swishing through files and links. "We're right in the center of the ship. And there's a cargo deck below us, so any kind of atmo leak would have to breach that, too. We'd be in space dock if that happened."

"Can you open it?" Joan asks.

"Yeah, just give me a minute." I work for a while in silence. "Actually, you could probably put a foot through the wall here, and we could just walk in. These interior walls are not very thick."

"I thought ships had all kinds of airtight bulkheads everywhere, so they can seal off parts when there's a hull breach." O'Neill shifts nervously from foot to foot.

"Now who's watching too many *Ancient TēVē* vids?" I joke. "There are airtight bulkheads every ten cabins. If you look back that way," I jerk my head back the way we came, "you can see where the vacuum barrier would slam shut across the hallway."

"And trap you here forever."

We all jump at the new voice.

"What are you doing down here, TC?" I turn to Joan. "Weren't you supposed to be our lookout?"

"No one assigned me any duties." Joan chuckles. "I'm just tagging along for the fun."

"This is TC," I tell the other two. "He's from the Techno-Inst on Kaku, doing an internship for his hospitality course. This is Joan and Ty."

They all bump fists.

"You all looked pretty guilty," TC says. "What kind of mayhem are you up to?"

I consider TC over the top of my holo. "You're probably better off not knowing. In fact, you might want to just wander away. We—" I indicate Joan and Ty "—all have other employment prospects."

TC's eyes widen and he grins. "Oooh, sounds fantastic. I'm in."

Joan shakes her head. "You were warned, young man."

"Got it." I flick a control, and the door whooshes open.

We crowd around the opening, peeking inside. It looks like a typical cabin. No noxious gasses escaping, no demolished walls, no pipes oozing green goo. Okay, I guess pipes oozing green goo was probably not even a possibility, but you get what I mean. It looks ordinary. The bunks are even neatly made.

"Let's get out of the hall," O'Neill says. Then he stops. "There aren't any alarms set, are there?"

"I already disabled them," I say smugly. "There was an alert set to notify someone if the door opened, but that's all I found. And believe me, I searched. Something that easy should have been a red herring."

We step into the room. "Who did the alert go to?" O'Neill asks. The door slides closed behind us. With four of us in the cabin, it's cramped.

"I'm not sure. It's a pocket file. I'll have to see if I can figure out who accesses it. Later." I step over to the bunks and stick my head inside the top one. "Nothing unusual here."

"Where did you learn to search?" O'Neill scoffs. He softens it with a smile and caress to my back. "You have to look a little harder than that. But carefully—we don't want to leave any evidence that we've been here." He starts opening drawers and pulling them out of the frame.

"Good thing we have a steward with us, then." I wink at TC. "He can make sure we get everything shipshape."

TC groans. "I knew I should have gone to the casino, instead."

Joan goes into the bathroom, and clanking sounds emerge. "No drugs hidden here," she calls out.

"You didn't mention drug interdiction in your background," I call back.

Her head pokes out of the bathroom and she smiles. "Need to know." She winks then disappears again.

O'Neill and TC have lifted the mattress on the top bunk on their side of the room. O'Neill slides a hand along the bed frame, under the mattress, then against the back wall.

I shrug and turn to the bunks on my side of the room. We work in silence for a few minutes, Joan's occasional calls of, "Clear!" coming out of the bathroom. I can't imagine where she is looking—those bathroom units don't have a lot of moveable parts.

"Got it!" O'Neill says, triumph in his voice.

"Wow," TC say.

"What did you find?" I try to peer around them. They're leaning into the bottom bunk and completely blocking my view.

O'Neill leans back. "There's an access panel here."

"What?" Joan crowds in.

O'Neill yanks the mattress the rest of the way out of the bunk and pushes it back to us. I wrestle it into the bunk behind me, leaving room for whatever may follow.

There are a few clinks and clicks, and the whoosh of an air seal. Cold air rolls up out of the bunk as O'Neill lifts the bottom. The thick metal panel hinges up on hydraulics and reveals a ladder.

"Does that go to the cargo level?" Joan leans over my shoulder.

"Where else could it go?" I ask. "That's the only thing below us."

"Now what?" TC's voice is high and his wide eyes excited. "Do we go down and investigate?"

"You have to stay here and guard the door," I say, just to see his reaction. His face falls, and I relent. "I'm kidding. I already set an alert on the door."

"Just make sure it's more effective than the one you disabled," Joan says.

"If anyone tries to disable it, I'll get a ping." I search my pockets. "Hang on, I have a glow stick here somewhere." I pull it out of my pocket and activate it.

O'Neill raises a leg to step over the bunk onto the ladder and pauses. "Check the OS and see if the cargo system has vids, T."

A wash of cold pours over me. I hadn't even thought about that. "It's a good thing I brought the pro along this time. I would have blundered in and set off all kinds of alerts."

TC beats me to the punch. "They've got cams with motion detectors. I can freeze them while we're down there and restart them after we leave. They'll never know anyone went in."

O'Neill looks from me to TC. "Are you two related? No offense, TC, but Triana, will you double check his work? This modification," he waves to the bunk, "was not cheap, which tells me something pretty shady is going on. We don't want them to know they've been busted."

I hand O'Neill the glow stick and flick through the OS. "Nice work, TC. This piece right here is genius." I indicate a particularly elegant line of code. TC grins.

O'Neill looks at the glow stick. "Why do you have this? Never mind. Can I drop it?"

When I nod, he drops the stick, and we all lean into the bunk to watch it fall. A couple meters below, it hits bottom and bounces slightly, the moving light creating crazy shadows. We wait, staring down at the weirdly glowing space.

The cargo level looks like any other cargo deck. Stacks of crates everywhere, with narrow gaps between. Directly below us, a pile of huge crates provides a landing for the short ladder. A gray rectangle lays next to the bottom of the ladder—a one by two-meter float panel.

I point. "That looks like it would fit perfectly into this bunk. You could climb down, activate the panel, and then ferry things up and down."

"What kind of things?" TC's voice cracks a little.

"Missing people?" Joan asks.

We all look at each other.

"Let's go see what we can find," O'Neill says, climbing down into the depths.

CHAPTER SIXTEEN

AS THE OTHERS climb down into the cargo deck, I rearrange the mattress on top of the hinged panel. I tuck in the coverings as well as I can and take a quick look around the room. I can't say we've left no trace, but if someone just glances in, they won't notice we've been here.

Double checking to make sure I can open the bunk from below, I climb down the ladder and pull it shut behind me. The others are grouped around the base of the ladder, waiting impatiently.

"Just trying to make sure no one will come in and realize we're here." I jump down to the crate.

"Good thought." O'Neill picks up the glow stick and leads the way across the top of the crate. "I think we can climb down over here." At the far end, there are a series of stacks forming a set of meter-high stairs.

"Is there some way to see what's in these crates?" TC asks. "Maybe they're stealing stuff from the hold?"

"Look for a CT chip." I look around the room, shining light from my holo-ring on the crates. I focus it on a corner near the stair steps. "See that little black square? That's the chip. I can read it with an app on my ring." I scan the crate. "Swintal Textiles bound for a distributor on S'Ride. Of course, that's what it claims. If someone is smuggling something else inside, we'll never know without opening it up. Or getting an internal scanner, and I don't have one of those."

"What?" O'Neill grins at me. "I thought you had every kind of tech."

I roll my eyes, hoping he can see it in the dim light. "IntScans are about three meters high and you have to push the crate through it, so I don't think I have room for one in my compartment on SK2. Much less the tiny drawer in my berth here."

"I have this vague memory of some kind of Nanobot scan," Joan says. "Of course, that was probably classified, so I'm going to have to kill you all, now."

We laugh, but I see O'Neill give Joan a strange look. What that's about?

I flick a copy of the scanning code to the others so we can all read the chips. We climb down from the crates and spread out through the hold. There's no way to know where they've been moving stuff—zark! I scramble back up the huge staircase.

"What are you doing?" O'Neill calls.

"I had an idea." I crouch beside the float panel. "If someone is moving stuff regularly, they might have pre-programmed a path into this thing." I turn on the panel and pull up the settings. "Bongo!"

"Bongo?" TC asks.

"It's an *Ancient TēVē* thing," O'Neill and I say in concert.

The float panel rises straight up to the bottom of the bunk and stops. We stare up at it.

"That's not good." TC hops back up the stairs. "I guess if you were using it, you'd either call it from up there, or you'd come down here and ride it back up. It's probably waiting for the user to load the cargo and send the next go command."

"You couldn't have thought of that before I turned it on?" I ask.

"Where's the fun in that?" TC flicks a few things on his holo-ring. "Let me try a near field command." He pulls me aside as the panel starts dropping. "I sent the continue command."

"How'd you do that?" I demand.

He shrugs. "I just sent a general command to any device within three meters."

"That could have been disastrous," O'Neil says. "What if there were other float panels laying around here? It's a cargo hold, so there are probably a bunch." He turns quickly, scanning the area.

"Relax, captain," TC says. "I looked. And I used a directional command. It's all good." He puts out a hand as the float panel drops to our level and swings himself up onto it. "Come on Triana, lets ride! I feel like Aladdin!"

I hold up my hands. "I'll just follow along. I don't trust any float panel I'm not controlling."

The panel moves to a clear space between the stacks of crates and drops like an asteroid in double gravity. TC hollers as it falls, clutching the sides. The panel stops a few centimeters above the deck and TC's chin smacks into his knees. He cries out as the panel slides away down the aisle. "I bit my tongue!" TC whimpers.

O'Neill laughs and jumps down off his own crate behind TC. Joan and I follow, shaking our heads.

"He makes me feel so old," I say.

"I *am* old," Joan replies. "It's not as bad as you've been led to believe."

TC and his flying carpet slide down the aisle between the stacks of crates. I scan each one we pass and report the findings to the rest of the group.

"More textiles. Brandy. AutoKich'ns. Ooh, baking chocolate." I stop in my tracks, gazing up at the top crate on the pile.

"Baking chocolate is unsweetened," O'Neill says over his shoulder. "You can't eat it."

Joan's lips twitch. "He knows you, doesn't he?"

"Everyone knows I love chocolate. But, yeah." I continue to scan the crates, loading the results into a file in case it's relevant, later.

We come to a closed hatch, and the panel stops. Still making faces, TC hops off and looks at the hatch controls. "It's manual."

"Why would there be a manual hatch in here?" I ask. "The bots can't operate those—unless they're highly specialized. That means someone has to come down here and open it."

"You might have just answered your own question," O'Neill replies. "They don't want any bots opening it. Do the honors, TC."

The boy grabs the wheel and spins it. He leans back and pulls the hatch open. Frigid air whooshes out, making me shiver. "Freezer," TC announces.

"Really?" Joan mutters.

TC steps inside, and a light in the ceiling flickers on. We crowd around the open hatch, peering through. The room is full of unmarked crates, each one meter by one meter by two.

"Those look familiar." I point my scan app at the corners.

Beside me, O'Neill has gone still. "Those look just like the crates you found in Charlie Bay back on SK2."

CHAPTER SEVENTEEN

I FREEZE. No pun intended. "You mean the ones with the people inside? The frozen people?"

"Frozen people?" Joan croaks. "Who does that?"

TC's face turns green.

When humanity first colonized the stars, they used a form of suspended animation to make the long, sub-light-speed journey. This involved using drugs to lower the passenger's metabolism to near zero, and then taking the body temperature down to just above freezing. Survival statistics were dismal. I don't remember the exact numbers, but I know it would be a failing grade in school. When jump technology was created, putting people into deep sleep became unnecessary. As a result, most modern people have a deep-seated revulsion to the idea.

"We don't know," O'Neill replies. "The people we found recovered, but they had no memory of how they ended up boxed and shipped."

"How many of them are there?" I ask, my throat constricted.

TC takes another look behind him and hurries back the way we came. A second later, we hear retching.

I step through the door. The boxes are stacked three high. I shine a light between the stacks, trying to see the back of the room. "I think there are at least twenty-one. Zark! I hope there isn't another row back there!" I hurry back out, my teeth starting to chatter.

"What do we do?" Joan whispers. "We can't just leave them. Your friend might be in there!"

O'Neill exits the freezer and carefully shuts the port behind him. "We can't just let them thaw, either. The docs on SK2 thought the memory loss might have been due to mishandled revival. They sat out in the cargo hold, melting, for hours. They might have recovered completely if they'd been revived properly."

"Yeah, but who knows how to do that?" I ask.

O'Neill shrugs. "Presumably the person responsible for their current state. So, we need to find out who put them here. And where they are going."

"How are we going to do that?" I ask.

He shakes his head. "Good old-fashioned investigation, I guess. Where's TC?"

"Here," a strangled voice says behind me.

"Not to be insensitive, but you didn't throw up, did you? We can't leave any evidence behind." O'Neill peers over TC's shoulder.

"I kept it down," TC mutters.

"Good." O'Neill turns and looks us over, then starts snapping out instructions. "TC, see if you can get that float panel back where it started. Joan, take a look around and make sure we didn't leave any evidence. Triana, can you set some alerts on that door, so we'll know if it opens again? Vid would be great, but just a notification would work. I'm going to see if there's anything else going on down here."

We all set to work, while O'Neill stalks away, prowling through the cargo hold. He returns as I'm putting the finishing touches on my program. "I've inserted a copy and divert command into that cam." I point up to the cam just outside the freezer. "And another in the cam inside. There aren't any electronics in this door, so the cams will have to do. I've also added some code to let me know if anyone tries to disable the cams like we did. I'll start them back up when we get upstairs."

"Can you get audio?" he asks.

I think for a moment. "I didn't see any audio pickups. I could come back with some equipment and set it up."

"No. Not worth the risk. Alerts and vid will have to do. There aren't any more of those." He jerks his chin towards the freezer. "But there are some small stashes of other contraband scattered around the hold. I'm not sure it's anything out of the ordinary for a ship like this, though. Probably put there to distract potential inspectors from noticing the people."

I stare at him. "It's a whole freezer full of people! How could anyone *not* notice it?"

He shakes his head. "I'm sure when we get closer to the port, they'll stack other things in front. Did you notice the crates are pushed to the back of the room? Easy to hide with a holo generator and some legitimate frozen items. Especially if the inspector finds the expected stuff out here. The only place they're in danger of an inspection is in port, anyway. It's not like there are roving bands of inspectors patrolling the galaxy."

I start to giggle, imagining pirates turned into government flunkies, stopping ships, and demanding to see their manifests.

"I enjoy macabre humor as much as the next Marine," Joan says. "Care to share?"

"Argh! Hand over yer paperwork, or I'll slit yer throat." I shake my head. "It was funnier inside my head."

Joan gives me an exaggerated look of concern. "I think you need a trip to the mind spa."

I hold up my hands to ward her off. "Nope, nobody is messing around in here." I tap my temple. "I'm good. I think we just need to get out of this hold."

O'Neill takes a last look around to make sure everything is back in place. "Let's get out of here. Triana, check the cabin."

"It's clear." I flick the holo closed. Ty gestures for TC to lead the way.

We climb up through the bunk and into the cabin. "Let's find somewhere we can talk without worrying about body snatchers bursting in on us," O'Neill says.

"Let me check the passageway before you open that." I put out a hand as Joan reaches for the door panel. While I pull up the corridor cams and preset the alerts, TC tidies up the cabin. It actually was a good thing he came along. O'Neill had made the bunk up all wrong.

"We're clear." I nod to Joan to open the door. "Let's go to Ty's place."

We slip out of the cabin and drift silently down the hall. Well, O'Neill and Joan drift silently. TC and I make enough noise to wake the people in the cargo freezer. "Sh! Why are you humming?" I ask him.

TC claps a hand over his mouth. "Sorry, I do that when I'm nervous." He makes a face at me.

I slap a hand over my own mouth, trying to stifle my nervous giggles. And then I trip over my own feet.

O'Neill catches me. "Good cover. If anyone finds us down here, you two are obviously drunk."

TC starts to protest, and I punch him in the arm. Joan rolls her eyes.

Fortunately, this section of B Deck is completely deserted. We stumble back to the float tubes and take them up. On the N Deck we step out into a crowd of passengers. Noises from the casino filter into the lobby, and a waitress offers us drinks as we stroll by. Around a corner, the sound disappears as we enter the cabin section. A few passengers wander through the passageways, but we make it to the Maia Suite without encountering anyone else.

"Did you disable the vids from here?" O'Neill asks as he opens the door.

I shush him and wave everyone inside. Once the door is closed, I smile. "Of course. As soon as I realized they were recording the private spaces." I don't tell him I've got the vids saving into my memory pocket. We can talk about that later.

While Joan and TC admire the view, O'Neill and I dial up some drinks. The ship is dropping down into the planetary plane, and out to the S'Ride orbit. We're not on the sun-ward side of the ship, so we get a great view of deep space. As we get closer, Sally Ride will come into view a few hours before we slide in to dock at Station Crippen-Hauck.

"So, what's the plan?" TC grabs a soda and plops down on the loveseat. "How we gonna bust some body snatcher butt?"

Joan sits in the plush armchair. "I could get used to this passenger thing. How'd you get this gig?"

O'Neill smiles. "I'm travelling for SK2 Board Security. It can be pretty sweet when it's not completely stressful."

"He's the best schmoozer I've ever seen," I tell Joan. "That's what it takes to be successful in board security." I look at her, considering. "With your background, you could probably get hired on at SK2. They're always looking for good security folks. If you ever want to give up the glamorous life of an itinerant dance instructor."

"The great food and travel are the main reasons I do this. Plus, I love dancing." Joan settles back into the chair. "I never wanted to commit to a station because I don't like to stay in one place that long."

"Most of my travel is to the planet—this is my first cruise." O'Neill takes the beer from the AutoKich'n and offers it to Joan. "I took a fast military scout to Armstrong once. This is much better."

"So glad you all can discuss your careers," TC interrupts, "but what about the frozen people in the hold?"

O'Neill drops down onto the sofa next to me. "I'll send an encrypted message to the docs back on SK2. They'll be able to tell us if there's a safe way to revive them. I think that would be the best possible answer—if we could just wake them up and they walk off the ship at SCH. If they don't suffer any memory loss, they can even tell us who put them in there."

"This is going to sound crazy," Joan says slowly. We all look at her. "What if they're there by choice? I mean, we don't have any proof your friend—"

"Les," I supply.

Joan nods. "Les. We don't know she's in there. And even if she is, maybe she's there voluntarily? Maybe it's a way for her to relocate or escape a bad relationship, or..." Her voice dies out. "I said it was crazy."

O'Neill holds up a hand. "We should look at all the possibilities. But even if they're there voluntarily, shipping people like ice cream bars isn't legal."

My stomach growls. Everyone turns to look at me. "Sorry, my stomach is very open to suggestion. You said ice cream. Are you sure shipping people is actually illegal? I mean, we're in interplanetary space, right TC?"

The boy nods. "We don't cross the Planetary Perimeter until Friday afternoon. About sixteen hours before we dock." He shrugs at my look. "Sixteen hours is pretty standard for cruise ships to cross the line. They all follow the same vectors."

"Interplanetary doesn't mean lawless," Joan says. "The Galactic Human Rights Standards still apply. I'm pretty sure freezing someone against their will violates the bodily harm statutes. But I'm still wondering about voluntary participation. I mean, the first colonists from Earth came out here exactly like that."

"Not exactly," I say. "They weren't hidden in a cargo hold on a cruise ship."

"I think we can all agree there's something off with the whole situation, voluntary or not." Ty looks at me. "Did you try scanning any of those crates?"

"Yeah." I shake my head. "They said frozen vegetables."

Everyone groans.

"Okay, so at a minimum, we're talking about improperly documented immigrants. Worst case is slavery." O'Neill scrubs his hands through his hair.

"Or invasion!" TC lolls back in his chair. "Like a Trojan Horse kind of thing."

"Unless they're some kind of genetically modified super soldiers, I don't think twenty-one people is really an invasion," I reply.

"What if they're carrying some kind of weaponized virus?" Joan asks. We all turn and stare.

"That's a terrifying thought," I say. "But modern medical technology can handle pretty much any virus, right?"

TC sits up. "This could be the start of the zombie apocalypse!"

I throw a pillow at him.

"Another reason not to revive them without adequate medical supervision," O'Neill says. "I guess we need to find out if the ship's docs can handle that kind of threat."

"You want to know if the ship's docs can cure zombies?" Joan asks with a smirk.

O'Neill rolls his eyes. "You're a bad influence," he tells me.

"Hey, I'm not the one who brought up zombies!" I say indignantly. "And Joan and I just met. How can I have influenced her already?"

"I am insulted!" Joan says, throwing her arms out dramatically. "I was perfectly snarky before I met Triana, I will have you know!"

O'Neill jumps up from the couch and crosses to the AutoKich'n. "You three are driving me to drink. I hope you're happy."

TC throws the pillow back at me. "She is a bad influence. Look at me, an innocent intern, corrupted by her—" He waves his hands around. "I can't even complete a sentence anymore."

"I am going to smother you with this pillow, if you don't tone it down." I brandish the gold and beige striped cushion.

O'Neill grabs his second beer and stalks back across the room. "Let's get this figured out before this becomes a free-for-all. Triana, can you check the vid logs for that freezer, and see if you can figure out who's moving the bodies in there?" I nod and he continues. "At this point, that's about all we can do. We don't want to revive anyone without medical supervision, and who knows if the docs here are up to it."

I raise a hand. "I'm going to bet they aren't. There are two docs on this ship—an orthopedic and a general practitioner. I don't know about the GP, but the ortho needed my help to program nanobots for a simple sprain. That's basic ortho training. She wasn't even sure how to administer them. I don't know how she got through medical school."

"The GP is here because he's a drunk and can't get a job anywhere else," Joan says. "Or at least that's the rumor. I know he's good at handing out pain patches, but that's about it."

"I just ran a scan on the vid feeds from that freezer." I dim the window and throw the vid up onto it. It shows the freezer we just left with its twenty-one long, rectangular boxes. "There are significant gaps in the coverage. They've tried to hide it by looping a pre-recorded vid into the feed. Basically, they're disabling the cam every time they move something in or out. Like we did."

I flip to another view. Stacks of crates fill much of the picture, but the freezer door is clearly visible at the back of the space. Bots move around the room, shuffling crates. "Here's some activity outside the freezer, when they docked on SK2. The freezer hatch never opens. But watch this crate." I point to a small box in the bottom corner of the screen, then slow the vid to quarter speed. A brief flicker, almost too fast to see, ripples the vid. "It's gone. So, obviously, someone deleted part of the recording."

CHAPTER EIGHTEEN

O'NEILL SCRUBS A HAND over his face. "That means someone with access to the vid feeds is part of this. Can you put together a list, T?"

"Ollie's supposed to be getting me that. It's going to be pretty long." I rub my forehead. "I feel like we're missing something obvious."

"Maybe we need to take a break," O'Neill says. "We can't help those people right now, and nobody can leave the ship until we dock at SCH, so we have a couple days. We've set everything in motion that I can think of."

"Can we finally go dancing?" Joan asks.

TC grimaces. "Don't you ever take a break from that?"

"I'm a dancer." Joan jumps up from her seat. "I do it because I love it. Come on, it will be fun. And the exercise will make our brains work better." She grabs TC's hand and dances him around the room. "Relax! Let me lead."

I pull my legs up onto the couch as they stumble by, hoping they don't fall on me. Even with Joan's expert leading, TC does not follow well. "He might need some remedial training," I whisper to O'Neill.

Since Joan is clearly not to be deterred, we deposit the glasses in the AutoKich'n. Joan stops us before we head out the door. "Wait! We need to change. TC, go put on your flashiest party clothes. Triana, I'm betting you haven't got anything besides uniforms and sweatpants with you."

O'Neill laughs. "Maybe not sweatpants, but I'm sure she doesn't have anything very fancy. My girl is all about comfort." He smiles and gives me a kiss on the cheek.

I wrinkle my nose. He's right, of course, but I'm not sure how I feel about this. Maybe I should make more of an effort, once in a while.

"You're coming with me," Joan says. "I have the perfect outfit for you."

"But we are supposed to wear our uniforms when we're in passenger spaces," I protest. "Not that this is comfortable or attractive, but rules are rules."

Joan waves that away. "When you're dancing, your uniform is dance clothes. Even if you're off duty. I've got you covered. Come on. Ty, TC, we'll meet you on H Deck by the float tubes."

Joan takes me to a cabin on D Deck. "This isn't my cabin—I'm the next one." She points down the hall. "This one's been converted to costume storage." She waves the door open.

We step into a room a little larger than mine, but instead of bunks, there are rows of head-high clothing racks filling the space, all of them packed with brightly colored costumes. Joan gives me a quick once-over, then flicks a switch on the nearest rack. It rises up off the floor about four centimeters, and she pushes it aside, making an aisle between two of the racks. Flipping the switch again settles it back to the floor, and she steps forward into the gap.

"These should fit you." She slides hangers aside, one after another, paging through the glitzy dresses. "No red. This won't work. Nope. Ew, who thought this was a good color? Puce? Really? No. Maybe. Nope." Finally, she pulls a hanger from the rack. "This one."

She holds a gold and green dress against my chest. The bodice is low cut but not too plunging, and it has transparent silk in the cleavage. "Dance dresses have to keep the important bits covered, even when you're twisting and bending," she says. "This transparent silk is smart fabric—it matches your skin tone." She holds her hand behind the clear bit, and it takes on a pale beige, matching her hand. "This green will look fabulous with your red hair. Go ahead, try it on. I'm going to pick one for myself."

She moves a couple more racks out of the way, foraging for another costume. I take a moment to make sure the cams in this room are temporarily disabled and unfasten my Pleiades line coverall. The dress slides over my head, smooth and silky to the touch, nothing like the costumes I remember from childhood dance recitals. No poky netting or scratchy lace, just soft silk and surprisingly comfortable sequins.

The full, metallic gold skirt ends just below my knees and bells out into a circle when I spin. "Bravo!" Joan applauds. She's dressed in flowy, floor length black pants and a form-fitting top with a jaunty little jacket in red. A tiny, red hat sits on top of her silver-blonde head. She holds out a pair of sparkling green dance shoes. "See if these fit. They've got smart-fit technology, but they only adjust to a small range of sizes."

We leave our clothes in the costume room. "No one will be in here tonight. All the competition fittings have been done." She leads the way up to the H Deck.

When we step out of the float tube, O'Neill and TC are waiting for us. TC's jaw drops. He's wearing his gold shirt and black pants again. "Wow." He looks from me to Joan and back. "I should have had Joan dress me! You both look like vid stars. Except your hair."

I put a hand up to my head.

Joan's face falls. "Yikes! We forgot hair!" She drags me into the ladies' room. "I don't know what I was thinking!" Without waiting for me to answer, she shoves me into the Insta-Transform booth at the end of the room. "Don't worry," she calls, "I've got it set to naturally curly."

I close my eyes and grit my teeth as the hair-bots move toward my head. "I hate these things."

"If they're set right, they're great. "These high-end ones have different hair textures. When you're curly, you don't want to use the cheap ones, for sure."

With a minimum of hair pulling, the thing does its job, and the door opens. "Much better," Joan says.

I look in the mirror. While my hair doesn't look as good as when Kara does it for me, it's not bad. The frizz has been contained, and the curls look intentional rather than caused by atmospheric conditions. "You're lucky," I say, eyeing Joan's short, spiky silver hair.

"You could do this, if you wanted!" She ruffles her fingers through the locks, perking up the strands.

"Maybe, someday."

We troop back to the lobby.

Ty looks spectacular in his *tux-i-doo*. "You look like a dream," he whispers, sliding an arm around my waist. Warmth washes up through my stomach and chest and into my face. "And I prefer your hair kind of crazy."

Joan takes us to the Taygete Lounge. We find one of the few empty tables near an inner wall and order drinks.

"What's the Taygete Special?" TC asks the automated table menu.

"The Taygete Special is a blended, frozen drink with fruit juices, Farberian Rum, Lecertes Vapor, and a squeeze of our own custom distilled Pleiades Liquor," an androgynous voice replies. "Do you require a complete list of ingredients or nutritional information?"

"No. I'll try one." TC looks at the rest of us. "If Joan is going to make me dance, I'd better get some muscle relaxant going."

Joan shakes a finger at him. "Not too much alcohol! You need just enough to drop your inhibitions without impairing your motor control. It's a fine line."

"I wonder if that's something you could calculate," I muse. "You'd need to know body mass, alcohol absorption rate—"

Joan cuts me off. "It's an art, not a science. I'm pretty good at finding the sweet spot."

We order three more of the drinks and watch the dancers while we wait. This cruise really is a dance cruise. A dozen couples take the floor for each dance. Some of them are pretty spectacular, while others are spectacularly bad.

"That's a perfect example of how not to dance." Joan juts her chin at a large woman in a bright pink suit. She steers her partner, a tiny man in drab robes, around the floor like a cargo bot moving crates. Frightened dancers dive out of the way as the couple approaches, darting between tables to avoid the collision.

"In ancient times, dancing was a gendered sport," Joan says. "Men led, women followed. Period. Now you can learn to lead or to follow, or both. And just dance whichever part you want. I prefer to lead." She pauses and smiles as the drink bot arrives. "Thus ends the lecture portion of the evening! Drink up and let's dance!"

She waits for TC to take two gulps of his beverage before hauling him out onto the floor. The pink woman has retired for the moment, leaving plenty of room for TC to trip over his own feet. Joan patiently guides him around the periphery of the space, stopping to demonstrate moves and giving him instructions.

O'Neill and I sit back and watch in companionable silence. At the end of the second song, a woman cuts in, and TC scurries back to our table. He wipes the sweat from his face with a napkin, and gulps down half his glass.

"She's a great teacher, but that dancing stuff is exhausting." TC pants between words. "Left, right, back, forward. I don't know how they make it look so easy!" He gestures to Joan and her new partner. The woman's peach outfit clashes with Joan's red, but there's no doubt she's a good dancer. They slide and spin effortlessly around the room. Seeing their skill, others move to the edges, to give them space. Joan swings the woman into a series of spins, lifts, and drops. When the song ends, the room breaks into applause.

As the next song starts, O'Neill offers me a hand. "Ready to give it a try?"

I slide off my stool and take his hand. The music soars around us and Ty sweeps us into a smooth, gliding dance. I relax and let my body remember all those years of dance lessons, back when my mother insisted on deportment classes. Ty's arms hold me close, the air between us electric. He gazes down at me as we spin, and it feels like the entire universe is locked out of our beautiful bubble of movement.

The song ends too soon, and the band picks this moment to take a break. Can't they see I need another song?

When we return to the table, Joan applauds. "I knew you could dance! You move so naturally. When you aren't tripping over your own feet, of course."

I smile. "I can dance. My mother insisted. But I'm not performing."

Joan holds up a hand. "You don't have to. Ambar would kill us all if I tried to replace her. More's the pity." She shakes her head.

"Would one of you lovely ladies give me the honor of the next dance?" A nasal voice comes from behind me. A tall, thin man with a young face, ancient eyes, and spiky green hair stands there. His voice is cold and assured, as if no one would dare to turn him down.

"Sorry," I say over my shoulder. "Joan and I are resting. I'm sure TC would be happy to honor you." I turn back to the table and pull a face.

TC chokes on his drink. "I'm not very good."

The creepy guy holds up a hand. "Perhaps another time, then."

"Who was that guy?" O'Neil asks as he walks away.

I tell them how I landed in his lap on my trek across the StarDeck on that first night. "He seemed to think I should be thrilled to find myself on his knee. Zarking top-levs."

The corner of O'Neill's lip twists. "We all know how those top-levs are."

I smack his arm. "Hey, I can say it. You can't."

Joan gives us a considering look but doesn't ask. We sit and watch Ser Skeevy work his way across the room, chatting up every attractive woman. When the music restarts, he steps onto the dance floor with one of them. "She looks young enough to be his granddaughter."

O'Neill shrugs. "At this distance, can you really tell? She could have had some work done, too. You gotta figure every passenger on this tub is an upper-lev—no one else can afford it."

TC is staring across the room. I wave a hand in front of his face, but he doesn't even notice. O'Neill nudges me and jerks his head toward the door.

Sandrine, one of the other interns, stands just inside the door. She's dressed in a floor-length black sheath dress with a slit up to the middle of her thigh. The deep plunging neckline reveals way more skin than I would be comfortable showing. Her dark hair is piled high on her head, and she looks stunning. In fact—I turn back to TC and realize that's exactly who he's staring at.

Looking back, I notice the green haired man has zeroed in on Sandrine as well. As soon as the music stops, he leaves his current partner and strides across the room. He says something, and she smiles and puts her hand in his. They sweep out onto the dance floor as the music resumes with a sensuous, earthy, pulsing melody. The green haired man pulls Sandrine in close and grinds his hips against hers. I can actually hear grinding.

"Do you hear that?"

Joan catches my eye and darts a look at TC. His jaw clenches and unclenches, and his nostrils flare. I put a hand on his shoulder. He jumps. "I—sorry, did you say something?"

"No. But grinding your teeth like that can give you a headache. You okay?"

"What do you mean?" He tries to pull off nonchalant, but it fails miserably.

"Scary dude is old enough to be her great-grandfather. I'm sure they'll have nothing in common."

"How do you know how old he is?" O'Neill asks.

"You can see it in his eyes. He's had a LOT of work done." I shiver. "Eighty-four should not look like twenty-three. And before you ask, eighty-four is a guess. But I'm pretty good at estimating the real age of top-levs. I've had plenty of practice." Another thing my mother insisted I learn, but that one took.

"I'm curious, now." I take a still pic of the guy. I load it into the facial recognition program I installed in the OS. "I wanna see how close my estimate is."

Joan laughs. "I'll take that action—I'd say he's ninety-five."

My ring pings, and I pull up the results. With a silent whistle, I glance around to make sure he's not nearby, and stretch the screen big enough for the whole table to see. "You win, Joan. Ser Skeevy is Rael Ambani. He's ninety-two. And almost as wealthy as the Ice Dame."

"Who's the Ice Dame?" Joan asks.

"My boss," O'Neill says. "Imogen Morgan."

"You work for Dame Morgan?" Joan shakes her head. "You poor bastard."

"I've heard of this guy." I scroll through search results on his name. "He's an open secret in the upper levels. He targets lower income girls and offers them a short-term contract—like a few weeks—with a promise of a lavish lifestyle and extravagant exit clauses. Of course, lower-levs can't afford lawyers, so they don't realize the high payout is only if they are injured or die. I guess a few of his victims' families have actually received substantial payoffs."

"We need to get her away from him!" TC announces suddenly, his eyes fixed on the couple shimmying across the floor. Their dance moves would get them jailed on New Deseret.

Joan leans close to him. "Isn't she one of the interns?"

"Yeah." TC sighs heavily. "That's why we need to rescue her. It's really hard to avoid sexual advances of passengers." His face flushes slightly.

"Has someone been hitting on you?" I ask, feeling protective. "I can help you with that!"

TC shakes his head. "No, I'm okay. I took care of it."

"Well, what are you waiting for?" Joan picks up her drink, smiling vaguely at TC.

"What do you mean?" TC gives her a confused look.

She shakes her head. "Oh, TC, I forget how young you are. But you're also a computer genius. Call her back on duty."

He stares. After a second, he closes his mouth. "You're the genius," he whispers. He flicks his holo-ring to life and logs in to the OS. Three quick flicks sends a recall to Sandrine, directing her to report to Ops. "It's probably deserted, so she'll just wait around for a while, and Ser Skeevy over there will find fresh meat."

Across the room, Sandrine starts. With a quick word to her partner, she steps aside and flicks her holo-ring. The old guy stands in the middle of the floor as if he owns it, watching her possessively. I barely know this girl, but the man's expression makes my skin crawl. After a moment, she returns to Ser Skeevy and talks quickly, her hands moving in short, choppy movements. He says something to her, and the two of them move toward the door.

"Triana, do something!" TC wails.

I turn to Joan. "Can you distract him?" She nods, and I point at O'Neill. "Rescue Joan, if she needs it, will you? I'll meet you at your place, later." Then I grab TC's arm. "Come on, we need to move!" Without waiting for him to respond, I drag him on an intercept course. The three of us reach the edge of the dance floor just as Sandrine and Ser Skeevy get there.

Joan steps forward, putting a hand on the creepy dude's arm. "Is it too late to take you up on that dance? I'll let you lead." She gives him a flirtatious look that catches me completely off guard. It's like she turned on a switch, and she sparkles. She smiles and Skeevy returns it.

"Sandrine!" I pretend surprise. "Did you get called back, too? Come on, we don't want to be late." I wave TC to her other side and slide between her and the old dude. I give him my best top-lev smile. "We'll make sure she gets safely to her duty station." I push past him and guide her to the exit.

Looking over my shoulder, I see Joan schmooze Ser Skeevy. O'Neill, still at the table, gives me a wink, then focuses on Joan.

"Rael was going to walk me down to Ops." Sandrine pouts, holding back as we tug her through the door.

"Why?" I ask. "No point, if you're going back on duty."

"How did you know I was called back to duty?" Sandrine asks, suspiciously.

I give her my best "duh" look. "Because we did too? Something big must be going on. Or there's some kind of glitch." Best to set some ground work for the inevitable result.

Sandrine looks from me to TC and back. "It's taken me the whole cruise to catch his attention. I needed more time to cement the connection."

TC stops in the passageway. "What do you mean?"

The girl turns and looks at him. "Why do you think I took this internship? I'm not going back to Kaku if I can help it. I searched the ship's databases and the net to find and target the most susceptible top-lev." She sweeps a hand down her tight-fitting dress. "Then I packaged myself in the most marketable fashion. It's the whole reason I'm taking this stupid hospitality degree—the chance to meet some top-lev and score a contract. Rael is my ticket to a better life."

"So, you know about him?" TC's voice is soft and forlorn. "He's, like, a million years old."

"He's also loaded," Sandrine says, her voice cold. "And he likes young, dark-haired women. The last three girls he contracted left the relationship with considerable assets."

"Assets? Or payoffs?" I give the girl a hard look. "Top-levs are pretty canny with their contracts. You might live well while you're with him, but most of them specify that what you leave with is little more than what you brought into the contract. I've heard stories that would curl your toes. If they left with money, it's because he was afraid they'd press charges."

She gives me a scathing look. "How would a janitor know anything about a man like Rael?"

"I keep my ears open," I say. "I've lived on SK2 a long time, and there are a lot of skeevy top-levs there. But do your own research." I turn to the boy. "Come on, TC, let's go."

Sandrine looks confused. "But we have to report to Ops. I'm not even sure where Ops is!"

I freeze for an instant. "Right, I forgot. It's this way." I lead them to the float tubes, and we drop to B Deck.

When we get there, I wave the door open. As I expected, the place is deserted. Random and Kindra have been gone long enough that the room has darkened into energy saving mode. "Hello? Anyone home?" I step inside, activating the overheads.

As the lights flash on, my foot slips and I flail around, trying to maintain my balance. Behind me I hear a gasp and a strangled scream. I'm not sure which one was Sandrine and which TC. My legs fly out from under me, and I land on my butt with a splat.

"Ow!" I put my hand down on the floor to push myself up. The deck is slippery, and my hand is covered in red. Slowly, not wanting to see where it came from, I look around. A glint of light catches my eye.

It's the overhead, reflecting off Ollie's shiny head, where it lays on the floor in a pool of blood.

CHAPTER NINETEEN

LET ME CLARIFY—IT'S not just Ollie's head—his body is still attached. I crawl through the puddle of blood. "Call a medic!" I press my bloody fingers to his neck. Leaving smears of red across his skin and shirt collar, I search for a heartbeat.

Nothing.

Nothing.

Wait! I put my ear to his lips and hear the faintest of breaths.

"Get a doctor here, now!" I cry.

"They're on the way," TC says. "Where's he bleeding?"

"I don't know!" I slide my fingers around his bald head, careful not to move his neck. "Maybe here at the back? It feels warmer and stickier."

"Ulllrrr." Sandrine bolts down the hall, her face green.

TC drops to his knees beside me and Ollie. "I've had first aid training—used to lifeguard at Ebony Coast in the summers." He strips off his shiny gold shirt and rips off a sleeve. Folding it into a square, he presses it against the base of Ollie's skull. "I don't want to move his head, but maybe we can stop the bleeding."

"I need to access the vids before whoever did this tries to delete them." I grab the remains of his shirt and wipe my hands. "Hey, this is surprisingly absorbent."

TC nods. "I know. Good thing I don't really like that one." His voice is wistful.

"I'm sure you can find a new one. And maybe the cruise line will pay for it, since it was ruined in the line of duty." I grimace, looking down at my beautiful green and gold skirt, now scarlet and sopping. "They aren't going to be happy about this dress, though. They'll never get all the blood out of it."

With my hands relatively clean, I flick my holo-ring to life. "O'Neill," I say, not giving him time to answer. "We need you down here in Ops, now. I don't want to corrupt any evidence."

"Evidence?" he repeats. "I'm on my way. Send me a guide slip, will you? I can't access the crew areas."

I send him the file and set the float tube check to allow him through. Passengers aren't normally permitted below G Deck.

"What happened?" a voice behind me asks.

I spin around as TC responds. "We aren't sure. We came in and the room was dark. When the lights came on, we found Ollie. He's alive, barely."

One of the medics takes the soaked piece of sleeve from TC, handing him a white pad. The woman does a double take at the gold fabric but drops it and sets to work. The other medic drags in some equipment. Over his shoulder, he asks me the usual questions. "Can you confirm his identity as Oliver Chatta— Chattra— Chattrakulrak?" He tries the last name three times before he gets it close to right.

"Yes, that's Ollie," I reply. "His float chair is over there, but I think we need to leave it in place until Security can do a recording."

The medic glances up. "Float chair? Oh, wait, here it is, on his records." As if his missing legs required confirmation. "Can you check the chair for any other medical equipment? His records don't show anything, but we need to confirm."

"I'm not a medical expert." I cross to the chair. "And I really don't want to touch anything until Security gets here. But it looks pretty normal."

"That's good enough," the woman says. "Pleiades Line is pretty careful to document medical needs. They know we need good data to treat people. Even crew." Her voice is neutral, but an odd look crosses her face. Is

Pleiades known for mistreatment of crew members? I really should have done more research before I accepted this job.

In a few minutes, they've got Ollie strapped to a float panel, with wireless monitors arrayed around him, and an IV in his arm. "We're going to move him to the medical suite," the taller medic says. "We'll report his condition to his supervisor."

"Uh, his supervisor is missing," I say. "Can you report to me?"

"What do you mean, 'missing'?" the woman asks. "How can someone be missing on a cruise ship?"

I shrug. "I dunno. But we haven't seen her since yesterday."

"Are you his coworker?" she asks.

"Yeah, Triana Moore, maintenance." I flick my contact details to her ring. "I'll be on duty tomorrow, so if you can just let me know how he's doing, that would be great."

"I'll post an update to his profile," she says. "It will go to his designated emergency contact and his employment profile. I can't legally do anything else."

I bite my lip. "That will have to do." I can always hack into his account.

O'Neill arrives as the medics guide Ollie, strapped to the float panel, out the door. He glances at them, the floor, and me. "Are you okay?" he asks, standing in the door.

My lips twitch, trying not to laugh at the concern for me warring with his desire to keep the evidence unsullied. "I'm fine. I'm not sure where TC got to, though."

"He's down the hall with the brown-haired girl." He looks around the room again. "Hasn't Security arrived? It took me forever to evade Lady Grandelle."

I scowl. "Her again? I thought the Grendel was done with you."

"Apparently not. I tried to steer her towards Don Ambani, or Ser Skeevy as you like to call him, but she's obviously too old for him."

"And not poor enough." I skirt the puddle of blood and peek out the door. Down the hall, TC is holding Sandrine against his scrawny, bare chest, comforting her. He glances up and gives me a brilliant smile. I give him a thumbs up. "Very manly," I mutter to O'Neill.

He laughs but sobers immediately. "Let's do a recording so we can start nosing around." He reaches into his pocket and pulls out a tiny device. After flicking a few commands on his holo-ring, he tosses it into the center of the room. The device hovers about a meter above the deck and rotates slowly, emitting a beam of light as it scans and records the entire space. Then it zips around the room, doing individual recordings under desks, behind the trash can, in the bathroom. Finally, it hovers over the puddle and scans multiple times.

"Infrared, ultra-blue, heat, magnetic," O'Neill says, watching the device. "It's a pretty sweet piece of tech."

"You carry one with you at all times?" I ask.

"It's small. And you never know when you might need a good record. Besides, since I knew you were going to be on this cruise, I figured I'd come prepared."

"Very funny. But, thanks. I wonder where those security monkeys are."

"We're here, and we don't appreciate being called monkeys." A tall, heavy-set man stands in the doorway. "What the hell happened here?" Behind him, a woman hovers, almost as tall, but twiggy.

Ty steps forward. "I'm Tiberius O'Neill from the SK2 Board of Directors Security department." He flicks his official ID to the new guy. "This is Triana Moore, currently detailed to CSS Morningstar Maintenance crew. She came down here with a couple interns, and they discovered the scene. I'm a passenger on this trip, but Technician Moore and I have worked together in the past, and she asked for my assistance.

"Technician Moore and the interns discovered Oliver Chattrakulrak on the floor, unconscious, in this pool of what we assume is his own blood. They called for medical help, and for you." O'Neill gives them a look up and down. "The medics arrived promptly and transported the victim to a treatment area."

The big guy narrows his eyes. "What are you trying to say? That we didn't respond fast enough? We were busy."

"With dinner?" I demand. "I checked your location when I called. You were in the Orion lounge."

"We were busy," the guy repeats, his voice menacing.

O'Neill holds up both hands. "You're here now. I've made a recording of the location using an SPD-35 recorder."

The woman whistles. "Where'd you get one of those? Pleiades only has the SPD-24s."

The man's head snaps around to her, then swivels back to us. When he turns back, she rolls her eyes. I bite my lip.

"I'm Agent Countryman. This is Agent DiFilippi." He jerks his head toward his companion. "I need that recording."

"I'll send you a copy." O'Neill flicks his holo-ring.

"I don't want a copy," Countryman growls. "I want the original. You have no need for it."

"Since I'm travelling on official business, and my employers own the Pleiades line, I am happy to assist with the investigation," O'Neill replies. I notice he doesn't agree to delete the recording.

Countryman growls again. "No need. DiFilippi and I can handle it." He turns to me. "Technician Chattrakulrak was on duty? Why did you come down here?" He doesn't even hesitate at Ollie's last name.

I shake my head. "Ollie wasn't on duty tonight. He and I both clocked out shortly after 6pm. Kindra and Random were on duty."

"Where are they?"

I lift my hands. "No idea. I came down with Tei Chaia and Sandrine. The interns. Sandrine got called back to duty, and since we were all together, we walked down. It was on the way to my cabin." I point down in the general direction of my cabin. Since I don't feel like manufacturing a fake recall for me and TC, this is easier. Hopefully, I'll get a chance to clue him in.

"You and this Tei Chaia having a fling? Isn't he a bit young for you?"

I feel O'Neill stiffen beside me, but I can't help laughing. "Me and TC? Are you crazy? I don't date children."

"Then why were the two of you going to your cabin?"

"*We* weren't. *I* was going to my cabin." I look at DiFilippi, hoping she's the more rational of the two. "TC has a thing for Sandrine, so when she had to come back to work, he wanted to walk with her. She's not quite so, uh, enamored, so I agreed to come with them, since it's on my way. We were in the Taygete Lounge."

Still half-hidden behind the bulk of her partner, DiFilippi nods. Countryman shakes his head, as if exasperated by my nonsense. "Why aren't you in uniform?"

Joan's spiky, silver head pokes around DiFilippi. "She was with me. We were doing some dance demos, and she needed to be in costume."

Countryman grunts. "Dance demos. You dance contractors do whatever you want, but employees should be in uniform."

"Check the contracts, my friend." Joan sounds unconcerned.

"I would like to check the vids for this room." I interrupt. "I wanted to do it right away, but Agent O'Neill suggested I wait for official supervision." I gesture to the two of them.

"We'll do that," Countryman snaps. "DiFilippi?" He points toward the console without looking at her.

"Actually, I can't do that." DiFilippi picks her way across the room to the farthest station. "I have to request that from a technician. Technician Moore, please log in and pull up the vids. I'll witness and record."

"No funny business, I promise!" I hold up my hands. Then I log into the Operating System. Where, of course, the vids are missing.

CHAPTER TWENTY

"WHAT DO you mean they're missing?" Countryman yells.

"Usually, that word means gone, not here, unable to be located," I say through clenched teeth. This guy is really rubbing me the wrong way. "In this case, it means about an hour and twenty minutes of the record have been deleted. Or maybe they were never created in the first place."

I throw the vid up on the big screen. "As you can see, Random and Kindra were here as scheduled. They left the facility at 22:13. Calls forwarded to their holo-rings. The cams went dark at 22:23, after ten minutes of inactivity, as programmed. It should have woken up when the next person entered the room, but for whatever reason it didn't. Or it did, and the vid was deleted. The vid restarts at 23:42, when TC, Sandrine and I entered." I fast forward through the blank time. The screen flickers, and the Ops Center appears again, as I enter, and the lights flicker on. I take another step and my foot hits the blood. Skirts flying, my arms fling out, my legs kick up and I land on my rear.

Countryman laughs.

I glare. O'Neill puts a hand on my arm, stopping me from launching myself across the room at his stupid face. Not really, but I want to.

DiFilippi's lips twitch, but she keeps her face neutral. "At least we have a record of what happened after you arrived."

I feel a flicker of relief. Countryman can't blame me for damaging the scene, since my movements are documented on the vid. Even the comically clumsy ones. I fast forward, bringing us up to the live feed. "That's all I've got."

Countryman holds up a hand. "I need to take this call," he announces. He walks across the room and steps into the bathroom.

DiFilippi rolls her eyes again. "He's such a pompous ass. You have no idea what happened in here?"

I shake my head. "I can check the vids in the passageway to see who came in here, but if they knew how to erase this vid, they probably took care of those as well." With a few flicks, I prove my point. The corridor vids show empty passageway from the time Random and Kindra left until Countryman and DiFilippi arrived.

"That's interesting," O'Neill says. "The cams in the passageway didn't restart at the same time as the ones in here. We should see ourselves on this feed, too."

"That makes me think someone restarted those cams manually, rather than just turning the motion sensors back on," I muse. "Someone must have been watching, and when they saw us come in, they realized they needed to restart the cams."

"Not us. Them." O'Neill points at DiFilippi and the bathroom door in turn. "When they saw the security team come here, they reset the motion sensors."

"Why do it that way?" I ask. "Were they just sloppy, or is there a reason they waited?"

"How were they monitoring us?" DiFilippi asked.

"Vid in the restaurant?" I start ticking off ideas on my fingers. "Cam in the next passageway? Monitoring the calls to security? Tracking your holo-rings?"

"They can do that?" she asks.

"It can definitely be done," I reply. "I've done it myself on station. Why don't you know that? Shouldn't that be part of your investigative skill set?"

DiFilippi laughs, a little bitterly. "Investigative skill set? We are basically security guards. We don't investigate. If investigation is required, it's left up to the local jurisdiction. And since we're still in interplanetary space, the local jurisdiction is no one. This won't be investigated at all."

O'Neill opens his mouth, then closes it. After a moment, he tries again. "You should get a new job—it obviously bothers you."

She shrugs. "That's the plan. I was hoping to get enough experience to get into the academy."

O'Neill nods. "If we work together on this, I might be able to put in a recommendation for you."

DiFilippi's eyes light up. Just then, the bathroom door opens, and her shoulders drop.

"The doctors say he fell out of his chair and hit his head. Case closed," Countryman steps back into the room. "Maintenance girl, get this cleaned up."

"His chair was way over there." I point at the middle console. "If he fell out of his chair, it would be here. Or here." I point at my feet then at the deck by the drying puddle of blood. "Or maybe there. But not parked over there with the brakes set."

"And he hit the base of his skull on something." O'Neill pulls up the recording he made earlier. "There's nothing here," he gestures around the puddle, "that could have caused that particular trauma. If he'd somehow fallen backwards out of his chair, he could have hit his head on this console edge." He points to the corner of the console then at a clean section of floor. "But he would have fallen there."

"He must have crawled this meter or so, and then collapsed, allowing the blood to pool here," Countryman says.

"Leaving no blood trail?" DiFilippi asks.

Countryman glares at her. "The docs say it was accidental. That's good enough for me. Moore, clean up. Everyone else, OUT!"

Joan starts to speak, but the security guy cuts her off. "I don't need to hear any crazy theories from you. Stick to your dancing!"

Joan holds up her hands. "I wasn't going to offer any crazy theories. I need a security report, so my pay doesn't get docked for her damaged costume." She turns her head just far enough that he can't see her wink at me. "Can you help me with that, Agent Countryman?"

Countryman heaves a heavy sigh. “Come to my office tomorrow. Right now, let's get out of here so the technician can get back to work.”

“I’m not working tonight,” I say. “I did a full twelve hour shift today. I’ll call Kindra to clean up. She should have been notified when the alert went out from here, anyway.”

The security guy glares at me. “I said clean it up, technician. You can call your friends when you’re done.” He herds everyone out the door then glares back at me. “What are you waiting for? Get to work! And get into uniform!” The door whooshes shut behind him.

I log in to the system and put in a call to Kindra. “You and Random need to come back to Ops. Ollie was injured.”

“Where is he?” Kindra asks.

“You need to come back to work! You’re on the clock, and it happened in Ops!” I disconnect. Then I dictate a report of exactly what happened tonight. I try to stay professional, but my frustration with Kindra and Random’s absence might come through. Then, without giving myself time to second guess the decision, I send a copy to First Officer Frankl. I’m sick of being the only one who cares about their lack of work ethic.

A ping on my holo-ring informs me O’Neill is in the passageway. I send an open command to the door. “I haven’t touched anything,” I say as he enters.

“Good girl. I want to get another look around before you start the cleanup.”

“I figured.”

The door whooshes open again, and Random and Kindra rush in. Random stops short, staring at the floor. “Wow. That’s a lot of blood. Is it all Ollie’s?”

Kindra smacks his arm. “You aren’t supposed to say things like that out loud, idiot.”

O’Neill holds up a hand. “Please walk around the edges of the room. We’re still investigating.”

Kindra gives him an up-and-down look. “Who are you? Did security finally hire someone competent?”

“Did maintenance finally hire someone who knows how to do the job?” DiFilippi stands in the doorway, glaring at Kindra.

Kindra grins, hard and cold. "Back off DiFilippi. I know you try, and you can't help it if your boss is a *window frame*. But this guy looks like he knows what he's doing."

I look at O'Neill, who's just standing there, and back to Kindra. "What makes you think he knows what he's doing? Because he's shiny?" I bite my lip. "I mean, he does know what he's doing, but you can't tell just by looking at him. No offense," I say to O'Neill.

His lips twitch. "None taken. My investigative skills are not based on my appearance. However, I *do* know what I'm doing, so I'd appreciate it if you'd all stay out of my way while I do it." He turns to Kindra and Random. "Would you be so kind as to log into the system? I need to retrieve some data."

While they do that, I move over to O'Neill's side so I can whisper. "I figured out what we were missing, down in the cargo hold. I should have tracked holo-rings. I can set up a program to track who went in and out of that hold, going back as far as we need."

"Wouldn't our bad guys have deleted that info, too?" He asks.

I shake my head. "They can try, but I've never met anyone who can hide all the traces. Even me. And I know where to look if they tried."

DiFilippi strolls over. "Can I help with anything, Agent O'Neill? I ditched Countryman. He's busy with paperwork. He likes doing that."

"Yes, you can help," O'Neill says. "What's your first name?"

"Sasha." She holds out a fist.

O'Neill bumps his knuckles against hers. "Ty. Do you have any investigative training, Sasha?"

"Only what I've seen on crime vids."

"No worries." He turns to me. "Triana, do what you were talking about. Let me know what you find out."

"Where's Joan?" I log in to the system.

"She went back to the club. Didn't get enough dancing, I guess." He grins. The smile fades as he turns to Kindra. "Send me your logs, starting when you signed in today. You, too, Random. I'm looking for anything unusual. Where were you two when Ollie got here?"

Kindra gives him a narrow-eyed look. "I don't know what time he got here, so I can't really answer that, now can I?"

"You left at—" he glances at me, eyebrows raised.

"22:13." I've gotten into the system and started sifting for the holo-ring tracking. Ollie pulled it yesterday, when we were looking for Les, so I dig deeper to look at his log.

Random and Kindra glance at each other. "We were on a call," Random says. "Propulsion problems, and I, uh, needed help with the, uh—"

"Don't bother," Kindra interrupts. "He knows we weren't working. He's smarter than Les. Or any of the other idiots on this tub. Besides, she probably told him." She jerks her chin at me.

I give her a bland look. "I didn't, but I certainly can." I start my facial recognition program, looking for Random and Kindra after they were supposed to have started work tonight. The system starts pinging softly as it throws stills up on the big screen.

Kindra looks at the pictures and grits her teeth. "Suck up." She turns to O'Neill. "We weren't doing anything wrong. Operating procedures allow us to leave Ops as long as all systems are monitored. Random had all the alerts sent to his holo-ring."

"Really," I drawl. "So, he was notified when I entered ops at 23:42? And it took you—" I look at the clock. "Thirty-two minutes to return here?"

"The system said you were here, so I didn't need to come in, now, did I?" Kindra says with a smirk.

"Except I was off-duty. I'm not technically authorized to be here alone when I'm off duty. You should have come down to see why I was here." I raise my eyebrows at her.

"Whatever. No one died," she snaps.

"Except Ollie might have, if we hadn't come in," I say softly.

She looks away, deflated.

"Why *did* you come down here, Triana?" Random asks suddenly.

"It's a really long story. But basically, Sandrine—one of the interns—got into a tight spot, so I sent her a fake recall." I realize my story doesn't sound very good, even though it's true.

"You hacked the OS to send a recall?" Kindra pounces.

"Don't be ridiculous." I clamp down on the tinge of panic in my chest. I don't care about this job, I remind myself. Maybe I'll get lucky, and they'll fire me. "I just sent her a personal text telling her to come to Ops. She isn't experienced enough to know that isn't how it's done." I don't mention that TC doctored the text to look like it came from the purser. "I don't think pranking an intern is a crime, is it?"

Random laughs. "That's a world I don't want to live in."

"Okay, people, could we please stop pointing fingers at each other, and see if we can figure out what happened to Ollie?" O'Neill's voice is hard, and my heart drops. Knowing the best way to get back in his good graces is to do good work, I go back to my holo-ring tracking.

I find the loops Ollie wrote, and the reports he pulled. Then I copy and adjust, setting the system to pull holo-ring data from anyone who entered Ops tonight. I start at 6pm, when my shift officially ended. It feels like days ago.

•18:22:12 Kindra Simatra Washington enters

•18:22:15 Random Garcia Jones enters

•18:28:02 Triana Moore departs

•18:28:14 Oliver Chattrakulrak departs

No activity for a while. Then:

•19:02 Kindra and Random leave

•21:38 Random comes back

•21:58 Kindra arrives

•22:13 Kindra and Random leave again

•22:45 Ollie arrives

•22:51 Les arrives

•23:42 Sandrine, TC and I arrive

"Les?!" I yelp.

O'Neill turns and looks at me. "What did you say?"

I point at the data. "Les was here. She was here at 22:51. Got here six minutes after Ollie did. And she never left!" I look wildly around the room, as if we'd somehow missed her all this time.

"This is the Les who was missing?" O'Neill asks.

"Missing?" Random and DiFilippi say at the same time.

"No one has seen her since yesterday morning. Now suddenly she's here in the Ops center." I swipe through screens of data, searching for something that makes sense.

"How could she be missing?" Random asks.

I ignore him. Her holo-ring is not showing up in the system. It suddenly ceased to exist after we arrived here in the Ops Center. What was it Ollie told me about rings? The best way to hide one is to flush it. I bolt across the room to the bathroom.

Of course, there's nothing in the bowl. And with the vids missing, there's no way to see who might have flushed it. It could have been Les. Or it could have been someone using Les's ring. But if they flushed the ring, how did they get out of Ops? I lunge back into the center.

"Does this door open without a ring?" I interrupt O'Neill's explanation about Les.

Kindra gives me a "you must be an idiot" look, but Random answers. "Of course. There's a manual pull on the right side, behind that panel. It's a fail-safe—in case we have to evacuate, and the power net is down."

I cross the room and pop open the hatch. Inside is a red handle labeled "Emergency Exit" and instructions: Pull handle. Exit room. I laugh, maybe a touch hysterically. "Is there a way to see if it's been used?"

Random comes up behind me and peers over my shoulder. I move out of his way, so he doesn't have to stand on his tippy toes. "It's definitely been used." He reaches out to touch the handle. "It should be up like this—"

"Don't!" O'Neill and DiFilippi cry in unison.

Random jerks back in reaction and his hand hits me in the face.

"OW!" I rub my cheek, moving out of the way as the two security agents crowd in.

"Sorry," Random mutters. "What did I do wrong?"

"I think they're looking for fingerprints or something."

"Much more than that." O'Neill has his high-tech whatever-it-was-35 out, shining some kind of light on the handle. He grunts in approval. "Micro samples of skin! Sasha, can you run these through the cruise line database?"

DiFilippi rubs the back of her neck. "I think so. I'll have to distract Countryman."

"I can do that," Kindra cries enthusiastically, as if trying to make up for her earlier obstruction.

Random gives her a warning look. "What are you going to do?"

She smiles. "You probably want plausible deniability."

We turn our backs to Kindra and focus on O'Neill and his wonder machine. "Heat scan shows it's cold, so it hasn't been touched in—based on the composition of the handle and ambient temperature of the room—probably thirty to forty minutes."

"We already knew that," I say grumpily. "We've been here that long."

O'Neill smiles. "Wait." He flicks his holo-ring and swipes through a few command screens. "Half-life decay scan of the skin cells indicate someone used this handle forty-seven minutes ago."

"Sec-lady!" Kindra calls out.

We all swing around. She's pointing at DiFilippi. "Countryman is on his way to the StarDeck. Now's your chance." She makes a "come here" motion with her fingers, and the two of them huddle over her console. O'Neill goes back to playing with his scanner.

"How did she distract him?" Random asks, nervously.

I start to laugh and throw a vid up on the big screen. The speakers shake with the sound of bells clanging and metal chinging. One of the slot machines on the StarDeck spews out credit disks. Passengers scramble around on the floor, scooping up the ship-board currency. More crowd out of nearby doorways, lunging into the scrum grouped around the machine. A couple junior pursers try to urge people away, and one of them gets a punch in the face.

Random shakes his head. "I don't want to know how you did that! I just hope you covered your tracks."

Kindra smirks. "Do what? You know those machines aren't tied into the OS. The gambling commission would go nova if they were."

"Uh, this doesn't make sense," DiFilippi says.

"What?" O'Neill's head snaps away from his holo. "Did you find something? Who opened the door?"

She rubs the back of her neck, again. "Ollie did."

CHAPTER TWENTY-ONE

WE ALL STARE AT HER. "He was out cold," I say.

She holds up her hands. "The system says it was his skin on the handle. Maybe he did it before he got whacked on the head."

"Or maybe Les used his hand to pull the panel." Random grabs Kindra's hand and pushes it toward the handle.

She yanks her hand away. "Yeah, because tiny Les could manhandle an unconscious Ollie up the wall like that."

"Good point," O'Neill says. "It's possible the skin cells were planted, but that implies a much more convoluted scheme than I'm willing to consider at this time. I think he must have done it before he got whacked."

"But why would Ollie use the handle?" I ask. "He had his holo-ring. He could just wave the door open."

"Did he?" O'Neill gives me a penetrating look. "Did you see his holo-ring on his finger?"

I think back, trying to remember. "I don't know. It never occurred to me to check."

O'Neill shakes his head. "No reason it should have. Can you locate it now?"

I swipe through the menus, pulling up the holo-ring tracking program again.

"This is probably a silly question," DiFilippi says hesitantly.

"Ask," O'Neill says. "That's how you'll learn."

"I've only met Ollie once, at the gym…"

"He practically lives there," Random puts in.

O'Neill glares at Random. He grins unapologetically, but shuts his mouth and mimes locking it with his holo-ring.

"If his float chair was over here—" DiFilippi points to the corner where the chair sits, deactivated. "How did he reach that panel?"

We all look at each other, nonplussed.

After a moment, Kindra speaks. "Maybe he opened the door first, then moved his chair over here." She walks across the room, demonstrating the path he might have taken. "Then, when he isn't looking, Les whacks him with something, and runs out the door." She swings her arms as if wielding a club, then dropping it.

"Except he didn't fall there," I say. "He fell over here, where the big puddle of blood is currently drying into the decking."

"Fine." Kindra goes back to the door to try again. She crouches down, then slowly stands. "He raised his chair to reach the handle, pulled it, and opened the door." She turns and makes an opening gesture with her hands. "Then he went over here, where Les whacked him. She moves the chair over there. For some reason. And runs away."

We look at the blood, then at the chair.

My screen pings. "Ollie's ring, and presumably Ollie, are in the medical suite. Here's the vid feed." On screen, Ollie lies peacefully in a white bed, his head wrapped in gauze.

"We know Ollie opened the door." O'Neill paces across the room. "We don't know why, since he had his ring on. Let's not worry about that right now. We really need to figure out where Les has been hiding and how we can find her."

I yawn. "I hate to be a party pooper, but I need to come back on duty in —" I look at the time. "Zark, a little more than four hours. I need to go to bed." I log out of the system and close down the console I've been using.

O'Neill nods. "Fair enough. Kindra, you can go ahead and start the cleanup. I've got everything I'm going to get." He pats his jacket pocket, where I'm sure the Magic-Evidence-Getter-9000 is safely stashed. "Maybe a night's sleep will jiggle things around to where they make sense. Sasha, if you think of anything else, let me know, will you?" He slides an arm around my shoulders and ushers me toward the door.

DiFilippi follows us out of the room. "I need to get back up to the office before Countryman starts looking for me."

"He's still busy," Kindra calls after us, her voice gleeful. "Can't get between a cruise passenger and a credit-spewing slot machine!"

The door swooshes shut behind us. We walk in silence for a few minutes. Then DiFilippi clears her throat. We stop and look at her.

"I'm not sure I should tell you this—"

"Either tell us or don't." I cover another yawn. "But don't do the 'if I told you, I'd have to stun you' routine."

O'Neill gives me a little shake. I'm not sure if he's agreeing with me or chastising me, but I'm too tired to care.

"When I was running Ollie's fingerprints." She stops, then tries again. "I saw something on Kindra's screen."

"What did you see?" O'Neill prompts. The man has the patience of a saint.

"She has an app on her home screen called VidDelete. What if she's the one hiding the evidence?" DiFilippi's eyes are wide and worried.

O'Neill turns to me. "Do you know anything about this app?"

I shrug. "No, but that doesn't mean anything. Maybe she uses it for clearing her personal vid feed. Or," I shrug again, "maybe it's part of the standard tool set. There's a lot of tools in the OS that I haven't even looked at."

"But why was it on her screen? Doesn't that mean she uses it?" the woman asks.

"I don't know," I say irritably. "If you're asking if I think Kindra is in this, then I have no idea. But she seemed kind of upset that Ollie was hurt. She may be lazy and manipulative, but that doesn't make her an Ollie whacker. I sure as heck don't trust her, but I'm not ready to point a finger at her yet."

O'Neill nods. "Why don't you go to bed, Triana. Sasha and I can rehash all of this information, and maybe come up with some kind of scenario. I'll see you in the morning." He kisses the top of my head, and strides away, DiFilippi on his heels.

I stare after him. He didn't invite me to come up to his cabin or walk me to my own. He just abandoned me in the middle of the ship to go have a confab with his new partner. Fantastic. I turn and look at the door next to me, trying to get my bearings. I wasn't paying any attention to where we walked.

The cabin door on my right says C-251. I guess he did walk me to my cabin. I go in and collapse into my bunk, asleep before Ser Grumpy can complain about the light.

THE NEXT MORNING comes way too early. Sim and Maarta are arguing over something when I stick my head out of my bunk.

"You're going to be late, girl." Sim smirks. "Partying all night is a no-no for good little staff members!"

I roll my eyes and groan.

"What time did you get in?" Maarta rummages in her drawer. "Do you need meds? I've got a hangover patch in here, somewhere."

I drop out of my bunk and pull a clean uniform from my drawer. "No hangover. Just not enough sleep. I need a shower. And coffee."

I stand under the sonic shower and turn it to "bright and early." After letting the waves pound my shoulders for a while, I stumble out and pull on my clothes. Maarta and Sim have already disappeared, so I lock my bunk and trudge out the door. Since I don't care if I'm late, I head for the dining hall. What's Kindra going to do, fire me? Besides, she owes me at least an hour already.

When I finally arrive in Ops, Kindra gives me a narrow-eyed glare. "Took you long enough to get here."

I roll my eyes. "Look who's talking. Who's covering for Ollie?"

Random shrugs and flicks some files at my console. "I guess you are. I can't do a twenty-four—it's against union rules."

"Union rules? Seriously? There's no union," I say.

"Maybe there should be. Anyway, if you don't like it, take it up with my boss." He logs out of his system and heads for the door.

"But she's missing!" I wail.

He shrugs. "Not my problem. Good luck." The two weasels slide out the door before I can respond.

Fan-forking-tastic. I'm stuck here, alone, and responsible for both ops and maintenance. Now what? Before I can even ask the question, a high-priority message comes in.

The next five hours are a blur. Broken fitness machines, plugged toilets, and malfunctioning vacu-bots vie for my attention with problems in propulsion and a navigational glitch.

"Navigational glitch?! I can't fix that! Call the station. They can send you a software patch. I'm a maintenance tech, not an astrogator!" I slam the bridge connection closed. If I didn't know better, I'd think they were just yanking my chain. Random probably put them up to it. I grind my teeth.

Around noon, I take thirty seconds to order a smoothie and check my messages. O'Neill hasn't called, and I haven't heard anything from medical. I sift through the OS and find Ollie's medical files. He's been given a complete med-pod treatment and was released back to duty a few hours ago. So, where is he?

I run the holo-ring tracker and find him. In the gym, of course. Apparently, he ignored the med-pod's orders to take it easy today. I call him. And get his vid-mail.

"I'm busy," his avatar says. "Leave a message."

I grind my teeth. "Ollie, it's Triana. I'm alone in Ops. Can you *please* come help me deal with all this—" I wave my arms around, trying to come up with a word. "Work? I need help, and the med scan said you're fit for duty. So please, come back." I sign off and debate calling O'Neill.

On the one hand, I want to know if he and Sasha—I think the name in a snarky tone—have found anything new. I hate being out of the loop. But I also hate feeling needy and whiny. I sit in my chair, bouncing my leg in indecision. Another item flashes red on my screen, and my chance is gone.

I'm about ready to pull my hair out by the time the door slides open and Ollie glides in. He's freshly showered and smiling. "How's it going?"

"How's it going?! I'm going to kill you. Then chop you up into little bits and jump up and down on them. Then suck those bits up with a damaged vacu-bot. Where the *fruit bowl* have you been?!"

Ollie rolls his eyes and ignores my question. "Any luck finding Les?"

"You found her. Or she found you."

Ollie goes still, then slowly turns his head to look at me. "What are you talking about?"

I point at my console. "Your holo-ring tracker said you and Les were both here at quarter to eleven last night. She must have whacked you over the head, but we can't figure out why you opened the door with the emergency handle."

He turns fully in his seat, staring at me. "What are you talking about?" he repeats.

"We came in a little before midnight. Random and Kindra weren't here—"

"No surprise there."

"But you were here, out cold on the floor in a puddle of blood. Don't you remember?" I flick my holo-ring to initiate a call to O'Neill. "Didn't you talk to security? Or my friend, the investigator?"

"No, soon as they let me out of the med-pod, I went to the gym," Ollie says, as if he gets hit on the head every cruise. Maybe he does.

"So, Les wasn't here when you came in last night? Why were you here anyway?"

"Why were you here?" Ollie counters.

I start to explain about Sandrine and the creepy old dude but wave it off. "Doesn't matter. *I* didn't get bludgeoned. You did. So, spill. Who hit you if it wasn't Les?"

Ollie stares at me for a minute then shrugs. "Don't know. I came in here to get my water bottle." He points at the metallic blue cylinder sitting on his desk. "Then WHAM! And I'm in a med-pod with a lingering headache."

I narrow my eyes at him. "Really? That's your story?"

He shrugs again. "That's all I got. Back to work."

"You get back to work," I counter. "I've been here for eight hours straight. I need a break."

"Going to the gym?" Ollie jibes.

"Yeah, right."

I find O'Neill and DiFilippi in the Asterope Pub. It's a little bistro on K Deck. Ty and *Sasha*—I really can't even think it without the sing-songy, teen-aged sneer—huddle in a corner booth, beer and fries scattered on the table between scratchpads and pens. I stalk over and stare down at them.

When I clear my throat, O'Neill looks up with a grin. DiFilippi glances at me and looks away. Does she think my name with a sneer, too?

"Ollie's back." I drag a nearby chair to the table. I drop into it and grab a fry. Not hot, but still tasty. I grab another.

O'Neill's eyes light up and his lips quirk.

A different look crosses DiFilippi's face, but I'm not sure what that expression was, it passed so quickly. She frowns. "Why didn't he come to see me? I left instructions that he was to come in for questioning as soon as the meds released him."

I shrug. "He went to the gym instead. Almost as if he gets whacked on the head every cruise. Besides—" I stab another fry into a dish of sauce. "It's not like you have any real jurisdiction."

DiFilippi's eyes narrow. "What do you mean?"

I raise my eyebrows. "Ship security isn't an actual police force. Besides, we're still in interplanetary space, so what laws even apply out here?"

The woman's eyes narrow further. "I have enough jurisdiction to throw you into the brig if you get in the way of my investigation. Corporate policy allows me to do that."

O'Neill holds up a hand. "She's not going to get in the way." He turns to me. "What did he say?"

I face O'Neill, as if DiFilippi doesn't exist. "He said he came back to get his water bottle, and he doesn't know who hit him. Not helpful at all."

"He didn't say anything about the emergency release handle?"

"Nope. And I didn't ask, because I don't want to get in the way of *your* investigation," I say sweetly, giving him a coy look.

O'Neill bites his lip. "Thank you. I think I'll stroll down there and have a chat with Ollie. You coming?" He pushes back his chair and stands.

"Yes," Sasha and I say in unison, jumping to our feet. Then we glare at each other.

"I'm going back to work," I say haughtily.

"May I assist you in the interrogation, Agent O'Neill?" DiFilippi takes a turn at the ignoring thing, but I see her glance at me out of the corner of her eye.

O'Neill gestures toward the door. "Of course. You had some really great insights."

She smirks.

I grit my teeth and lead the way back to Ops.

CHAPTER TWENTY-TWO

I'M ALMOST SURPRISED to see Ollie still at his station when we arrive in Ops. "These good folks want to ask you some questions about last night." I sign into my station and check the log. It seems to be working fine now—showing all four of us in the room.

While O'Neill and DiFilippi ask Ollie about his misadventure, I pull up the holo-ring tracking program and start running some checks. I set it to track Ollie, Kindra, Random, then throw in TC, Sandrine, Ambar, and Ser Skeevy, for good measure. After a second, I add Countryman and DiFilippi, too. Know the enemy, right? Setting the time frame back to when the ship departed Grissom, I let it run. With that much data to match and a ship this large, it will take a while.

"Why did you come to Ops when you were off-duty?" DiFilippi asks.

"Told her already." Ollie tips his head at me. "I needed my water bottle."

"You only have one?" the woman demands.

"Have you seen my berth? Only got room for one." He caresses the bottle. "Besides, it's my favorite."

I bite back a grin. Ollie has at least four other water bottles stashed in that cupboard beside his console, but I'm not helping *Sasha*.

"Technician—" O'Neill breaks in, giving DiFilippi a slight head shake.

"Can you tell us where you were before you came to Ops? Did anything unusual happen last night?"

"After work, the gym. Then dinner, and a vid in my berth. Remembered the water bottle and came back for it." He turns back to his screen and flicks a flashing red indicator. It slides off the screen. He glances at the two agents. "I'm on duty, you know."

O'Neill nods. "Sorry to distract you. Before we go, can you tell us if anyone would want to harm you? Do you have any idea who might have done it?"

Ollie shrugs, his massive shoulders rolling like a wave. "Docs say I fell."

"I understand the doctors on this ship may be slightly, uh, overmedicated," O'Neill says tactfully.

Ollie's lips twitch. "Maybe. But I can't think of anyone who'd want to whack me."

"Well, if you think of anything else—" DiFilippi flicks her contact info to him.

Ollie smiles. "I'll tell Triana."

I wink at him while Sasha grits her teeth.

Random and Kindra arrive at ten to seven, and Ollie and I clock out. The program I started earlier is still chugging away, but it can keep running without my input. I set the output file to save into my hidden data pocket, so I can check it later from another location, as long as I can access the OS.

Ambar, Joan, and O'Neill are practicing for their dance comp, of course. I snag a stash of snack food and stroll up to I Deck sending a vid call through to TC. "Wanna watch the Ambar show again?"

TC pouts. "I got moved to nights. I think Sandrine complained to someone, because I had a shift change posted to my account this morning. She's going looking for that Ser Skeevy, I know it!"

"TC, if she wants Ser Skeevy, she's not right for you." I shake my head. "Unless you're secretly independently wealthy."

What? It could be true. Exhibit A: Annabelle Morgan.

"No," he says mournfully. "Just the clothes on my back."

I laugh. "You should ask for a pay raise. Can you get away for a few minutes? I have food." I swing around a corner and head down the corridor toward the dance studio. From the far end, TC waves.

"There's always time for a snack!" He jogs toward me as I swipe the call closed.

When we're close enough, I toss him a muffin. It goes wide and splats onto the deck. TC laughs. "Good thing that was wrapped. Remind me not to pick you for the crew vs passengers dodgeball game."

I freeze. "The what now?"

TC slaps my shoulder, laughing harder. "You should see your face. I'm kidding. Although that would be awesome. I could pummel Ser Skeevy right in the stomach with one of those red, rubber balls. They hurt." He rubs his stomach reflexively.

"Can you open the dance studio door for me?"

TC smiles, waving his holo-ring at the door. A blast of music pounds out. "My pleasure, madam," he hollers. "Enjoy your stay."

I enter and sidestep towards the corner. Across the room, Ambar glares at me then turns her attention back to Joan and Ty. I lean against the wall, trying to stay out of the dancers' way. O'Neill spins Joan around the room, in a flurry of quick-steps, dips and turns. Joan holds up a hand and they stop, the music cutting off abruptly.

"Did you see the Alturan timing in the third measure, Ambar? That's what I was talking about. Make sure you do the switch step first, or you'll trip over your own feet, every time." She gently pushes Ty toward Ambar. "Try that part again."

Stepping back beside me, she gives me a wink then waves a hand and the music starts. "And don't look at your feet! They'll stay connected to your body, even if you aren't watching them."

Ambar's chin pops up as she puts her hand on O'Neill's shoulder. He slides an arm around her waist, and I feel a twinge of jealousy in my gut, which I heroically ignore. My good karma is rewarded when three steps into the sequence, Ambar trips and slams into the wall.

I bite back a smile. Joan starts forward. "Ambar, switch step. Let's go through it slowly." She takes Ambar by the arm and leads her to the center of the room. Joan demonstrates the step, then has Ambar go through it, one move at a time.

O'Neill strolls over to me. "That could have been you."

"Smashing into a wall?" I give him the stink eye. "I may not be a professional like Joan, but that—" I jerk my chin at Ambar "—would not have been me. I mastered Alturan timing in my teens."

"Really." Ty crosses his arms. "I thought you didn't dance."

I shake my head. "I said I don't perform. You know I can dance—we did it last night."

"Yeah, but that wasn't anything fancy." His eyes sparkle, and he holds out his hand. "Let's see your Alturan timing."

I let him lead me out onto the dance floor. His arm slides around me, strong and warm. He takes my right hand and pushes gently. My body responds automatically, stepping back on my right foot. I remember Master Boudoir, my dance instructor, his voice thick with his own invented accent. "No spaghetti arms! You can't feel his lead if your arms are like limp noodles! Make your arms into a frame, solid but with some give. Whichever direction your partner moves his body, yours goes with it." We glide around the two women in the middle of the room, swirling on the rising music. I feel the daggers of Ambar's eyes slice through me, and I give her a smug smile.

We swing back around to our starting point, bodies moving in rhythm. Then Ty raises his left hand and gives me a gentle push with his right. I pivot through our joined hands and swing around, my feet moving through the Alturan steps like clockwork. He spins me back into his arms and smiles. A wash of warmth flows down my spine, and I beam.

The music stops. "Exactly!" Joan says. "Ambar, did you see that? Ty and Triana, do that step again. Ambar, watch their feet." Joan makes us repeat the three measures again and again, pointing and explaining as we go. Ambar grits her teeth and watches, her shoulders up around her ears.

"Right. Now Ambar, try it with Ty." Joan waves the music on and pulls me away, leaving the floor open for Ambar. "Why didn't you sign up for the competition?" she mutters. "Coaching you and Ty would be a dream."

I hold up a hand. "I don't perform. Dancing is fun, but I have no desire to be the center of attention. In fact, even this was bad enough." I wave a hand at Ty and Ambar. "She's going to hate me more than ever, now."

Joan shakes her head. "She'll get over it. But you're probably smart not to partner with Ty. I've seen more than one couple break up over a dance competition."

A spear goes through my heart. "What do you mean?"

She waves a hand. "It's easy to be really mean to people we care about. When you throw in the stress of competition, some couples just can't take it. My sister and her partner split right after winning the Galactic Sector Pro-Am. They argued about every move, every practice, every performance. Perfect!" she cries, waving the music off. "That was exactly right, Ambar!"

Ambar preens, giving me a dirty look under her eyelashes. I roll my eyes.

Joan looks at her holo. "That's all for tonight. We'll meet again tomorrow afternoon for a quick dress rehearsal, then show time is at nine. You have your costumes, right?" She looks from Ty to Ambar. They both nod obediently. "Great! Dinner time."

While Ty sits down on the narrow bench by the wall to change out of his dance shoes, Ambar saunters over to me. "Stay out of my way, Moore. Ty and I are going to win this thing, and you can't stop us."

I hold up my hands. "I don't want to stop you, Ambar. I'd love to see you win."

She narrows her eyes, but I smile. Gritting her teeth, she stomps across the room to change her shoes.

Joan hides a smile and turns to me. "Kill 'em with kindness. Do you have plans for dinner?"

"I need to check with O'Neill," I say, starting across the floor.

"Have you got any new information on our," Ty glances at Ambar, "situation?"

"If you mean from Ollie, then no." I sit down next to him, my voice low. "But, my holo-ring tracker should have data soon. It was about 80% done when I left Ops." I flick my ring and pull up a login screen. "We're going to need a big projection space to see it all, though."

O'Neill nods at the mirror. "Will that work, or should we go up to my suite?" He pauses for a second then whispers, "You didn't invite Ambar to join us, did you?"

I snort. "Not likely. You didn't invite *Sasha,* did you?" My mean girl sneer comes through on her name, and I bite my lip.

He glances at me, his expression amused. "Nope. Just you and me, kid."

"What?"

"It's an *Ancient TēVē* quote." He looks disappointed. "You don't recognize it?"

"Sorry. You sure you got it right?" I stand up.

"Never mind." He leads the way to the door. "We're going to have dinner in, tonight," he tells Ambar and Joan, who are obviously waiting for us. "We'll see you in the morning."

Ambar huffs out a breath and stomps out the door without another word. Joan hangs back, waiting for the door to swoosh shut. "Do you have anything new about the people in the hold?"

"Not yet," I say. "But my search routine should pop out some data any minute now."

"We could order some food, and hopefully by the time we're done, it will be, too. I can meet my friends later." She raises a hopeful eyebrow.

I glance at O'Neill and shrug. "Maybe we *should* call Sasha, too. Get the whole team together." Putting good Karma out into the universe is *hard,* sometimes!

"We'll fill her in later," O'Neill says. "She's investigating other avenues."

I smile and say a quick prayer of thanks to the Big Guy.

Joan and I pull some chairs out of the closet while O'Neill orders the food. We're just settling into our seats when my ring pings. "Results are in!" I announce, flicking the data sheet up onto the full-length mirror. "I'm arranging these in a timeline from the beginning of the previous leg of the cruise up to this morning."

I fling the results up as I scroll through them, narrating as I go. "They departed Grissom on the 4th. We already know Les was in Ops all day, then ate, went to the gym and went to her cabin." The words ops, dining, gym, and D-47 pop up on the first section of mirror in blue, with times and the date annotated above them. I throw the rest of Les's activities—mind-numbingly redundant—up across the mirror, and switch colors to peach.

"Ollie is also a creature of habit—almost the same habits, in fact. Ops, Dining, gym, and E-27. He's got a little more variety in timing, but, hang on.

He went to B-186 on the first night out!" We all exchange a look. "What was Ollie doing in the cargo hold?"

"You know—" Joan chews thoughtfully on her pickled veggies. "That float panel would be super convenient for him—getting up and down into the hold."

I wrinkle my nose. "True. But you should see him go up and down a ladder—he's really fast. Faster than the chair can lift, in fact. All those hours of weightlifting pay off, I guess."

"Still, he obviously went into B-186, so we have to assume he knows what's going on." O'Neill points his fork at the mirror. "But then why did he get whacked?"

I twist one of my springy red curls, thinking. "Maybe he and his partner had a disagreement? Or maybe he discovered the scheme, and the bad guys decided to take him out?" I ignore the veggies and grab a cupcake.

"Either way, we need to be careful." O'Neill says. "We don't want them to know that we know until we have backup from the station."

"Right." I lick the thick dollop of chocolate frosting off my little cake like an ice cream cone. "Here's the data on Kindra and Random." Setting the bare cake aside, I flick data up onto the mirror like blackjack dealer. "During the day, they were both asleep, and they started each evening at Ops, but after that, all bets are off. Random spent part of each night in the dance studios up here on I Deck." I glance at Joan. "He said he was on a team before."

Joan nods. "He's one of the best crew dancers. He won the Grissom to Kaku comp."

"Kindra seems to have spread her time between all the different lounges on the ship, and Random joined her at some point each evening." Gray data pops up onto the mirror—darker for Kindra and lighter for Random. "Neither of them went to B-186, although Kindra went to D-47 on the last night, after the dance comp. Maybe she and Les were having a fling? That would certainly explain Les's willingness to overlook her regular less-than-professional work ethic."

"Hey!" Joan points at the mirror. "Les wasn't in D-47 on the last night. She was in C-126. How did we miss that before?"

O'Neill jumps up and we both rush to the mirror, as if getting closer will clarify the data. "Check which cabin Les was assigned to," O'Neill says.

I flick my ring and log into the OS. "C-126 is her berth. So why was she in D-47 all those nights?" I sift through more data and find the answer. "D-47 is assigned to some guy named Timmons."

"The purser?" Joan asks.

I dig some more. "Yup. The purser."

CHAPTER TWENTY-THREE

"NOW WE'RE GETTING SOMEWHERE," O'Neill says with satisfaction. "Les was spending every night with the purser, or at least in his cabin, until the last night. T, can you pull—"

"Already got it." I cut him off, flinging up a hand. "I'm putting a data grab around D-47 to track everyone who went in and out, going back to S'Ride—just because I can." I grin. "And yes, Timmons the purser is on day shift, so he was likely in his cabin at night." I let the data grab chug and turn back to the mirror. "If we assume Les was having a fling with Timmons, then he either dumped her or was two-timing her with Kindra—holy cow!"

"What?" O'Neill asks.

When I don't respond immediately, Joan leans forward. "Let me guess. There's a whole string of women visiting Timmons."

"How'd you know?" I ask.

Joan raises an eyebrow at me.

My eyes widen. "He hit on you? How does he still have all his extremities?"

Joan laughs. "Have you seen him? Maybe he doesn't."

O'Neill chokes on his drink. I thump him on the back.

"Don't get me wrong," Joan says. "He's a good-looking guy. If that were my thing, I might have jumped at it. Or jumped him, I guess I should say."

"Ugh." Ty makes a face.

"Yeah, the subject makes me queasy, too." Joan grins. "Timmons has a bit of a rep on the ship. Well, within the whole cruise line, actually. I was warned before I stepped foot on this boat. I figured my orientation would protect me, but that guy thinks he's irresistible to everyone. Has he hit on you, yet?"

"Me?" I ask in surprise. "I've never seen the guy, remember?"

"No." She nods at Ty. "I meant him."

O'Neill opens his mouth and shuts it again. Joan and I burst out laughing.

"Maybe he's learned to steer clear of the passengers," Joan says. "I've heard there have been some complaints, but the cruise line has settled them out of court."

O'Neill wipes his forehead dramatically. "Isn't that kind of odd, though? That Triana's never met him? He's part of the crew."

I scrunch up my nose, thinking. "It's not like I spend a lot of time with the other crew. Just Ollie. Maybe since I'm a temp, he can't be bothered? Or maybe the whole Les situation has him off his game. I mean, he must know she's gone missing."

"Maybe he's even responsible for her disappearance." Ty takes one of the cupcakes. Picking up a spoon, he scrapes off half the mountain of pink frosting and plops it onto my naked cake. "Someone once told me that a cupcake without frosting is just a muffin. And this is way too much sugar for me."

A warm glow tingles up my spine. "You really know the way to a girl's heart."

"Just looking at all that frosting makes my teeth hurt," Joan says with a shudder. She jumps up and points at the data on the mirror. "So, Les is dating Timmons, they split—did she dump him, or did he dump her? Does it matter? He takes up with Kindra. Did Timmons put Les in the freezer? Or did Kindra do it?"

O'Neill holds up a finger. "We don't know she's in the freezer. Although that does seem likely."

Joan waves, as if wiping a window clean. "Facts are so overrated. Let's make some assumptions. Timmons took up with Kindra. Les got pissed and confronted him. Maybe threatened to blow the whole operation. Timmons throws her in the freezer to keep her quiet." As she speaks, Joan acts out the whole sequence, her loose-limbed arms waving. "Now, if Ollie was in on the whole thing—and his visit to B-186 suggests he is—why did he get whacked?"

I eat the last of my re-frosted cupcake and wipe my hands as I get to my feet. "Ollie is the one who started me looking for Les. So obviously he didn't know Timmons was behind her disappearance. Maybe Ollie and Timmons had some kind of falling out, too?"

"Or maybe—" O'Neill stares at the data spread across the mirror. "Ollie decided Timmons was getting a little too dangerous. It's one thing to help cover up an illegal operation if you don't know the details. Or if you don't know the victims. But once the bad guys start taking out people you know, it gets a lot harder to stomach."

A shadow of a movement catches my eye. I stare at the mirror, eyes narrowed.

"What's up, Triana?" Joan asks.

"I thought I saw something." I mute the data projection and clear the mirror to transparent.

A woman stands on the other side of the wall, staring at us.

"Ambar!" we cry in unison.

O'Neill lunges for the door, Joan on his heels. Ambar bolts for the door in the opposite wall.

I flick my holo-ring to life and flip a couple icons. "Got her." I smile, smugly. "Locked the studio door."

Beyond the glass, Ambar waves furiously at the door, but it doesn't slide open. She turns and glares back at us.

I flick through the OS audio panels and activate a speaker in I-15. "What are you doing in there, Ambar?"

Ambar flips her hair over her shoulder. "I might ask you the same question."

I smile. "You might. But I asked first."

"Maybe I'm practicing some more. You all might think you're perfect, but maybe I want to put a little polish on my dance steps." She attempts the

Alturan timing and stumbles over her own feet. Flushing, she stares defiantly at us.

I sigh and mute the connection, turning back to the others. "Do you think she's spying on us?"

"Yes," Joan and Ty answer together.

"Could she see or hear anything from over there?" O'Neill asks.

"Probably not." I pull up the specs on the wall. "This brand of programmable window is supposed to be soundproof. But obviously they aren't completely opaque—I saw her move through the glass—that's why I checked to see who was over there. She might have been able to see some of what we were doing, but she shouldn't have been able to see the data."

"The real question," Joan says slowly, "is whether she's a risk. She's as unlikely to be involved in this as TC, right? And maybe she'll have some insights?"

"You don't sound too sure." I stare through the glass. "I ran a background check on her a few days ago. She seems to be mostly harmless."

Joan gives me a look. "You ran a background check? Why?"

I shrug. "It's what I do. I'm nosy."

O'Neill smiles. "T's snooping has saved us more than once. I say we bring her in."

How can I argue with those dimples?

Ambar stomps into the room a few minutes later. Arms crossed, she stands in the middle of the space, glaring at me. "We're having dinner in," she sneers, making air quotes.

"We didn't say where," I reply, mildly. "We've got lots of food left, if you're hungry."

She sniffs. "Why would I want to eat with you?"

Joan drags a fourth chair out of the closet and sets it next to hers. "Because we need your expertise." She locks eyes with the girl. "We've got an issue we can't discuss with the regular crew, and since you've got your finger on the pulse of the ship, we thought you might be able to help."

Laying it a bit thick, aren't you Joan?

Ambar flounces to the chair. "Well, I do have connections on this ship."

I stand corrected.

"We know." O'Neill leans forward. "You can give us the insider view."

Ambar relaxes a fraction and reaches for a bottled Sweet'n'Bublee. "I can't tell you any corporate secrets—since you two aren't crew—but I'll help if I can."

Turning my head so she can't see my eyes roll, I sit back and let the expert schmoozers do their thing.

"What can you tell us about crew, er, romantic liaisons?" Joan asks.

Ambar is a font of gossip. She knows all about Timmons and his parade of conquests. "I've heard he might even have had a discreet fling with the First Officer, but that one was kept really quiet—if it happened at all. But according to my sources, Les was just one of many crew he targeted for 'special assignments'. He propositioned me the first night out." She lifts her chin. "I didn't think it was a wise move. Plus, he's just not my type."

"You're a strong woman," Joan says. "Weren't you worried about your career?"

Ambar smiles, smugly. "Why do you think I leave this cam on full-time?" She waves to her name badge. "I want to make sure I'm being judged for my skills, not my unwillingness to *bookmark* the purser."

Zark! She's got the cam going!

O'Neill's head snaps around and he gives me a look. I hold up a hand and get to work on my holo-ring while Joan keeps Ambar distracted.

"Surely he knows that kind of behavior wouldn't be tolerated," O'Neill says. "Sexual harassment is pretty serious."

"I think he doesn't care enough to harass anyone. If someone says no, he just moves on," Joan says.

"We interns were all warned about him anyway." Ambar pays no attention to me madly swiping through screens. "The Techno-Inst instructors told us how to deal with harassment in general, and Timmons in particular. Apparently, he's kind of legendary in Pleiades."

I give O'Neill a discreet thumbs up. Ambar-cam feed diverted to my data pocket; all vid since she left the dance rehearsal removed from the regular system. At this rate, there's going to be weeks of vid in my pocket by the time we dock. I ignore an angry text from the reality show crew. "You're off-duty, right Ambar?"

She sits up straight. "A hospitality expert is never truly off duty," she proclaims. "But I'm not currently on the duty roster, if that's what you're asking. Why do you care?"

I shake my head. "Didn't want to interfere with your work."

She turns a shoulder to me and focuses on the other two. "Why do you want to know about crew relationships, anyway?"

Ty and Joan's eyes meet. "You understand this is classified," Ty says. "You know I work for SK2, which is part of the company that owns Pleiades?"

Ambar nods, lips parted in anticipation.

He gestures to the three of us "We are on an undercover mission for the company. We've heard there might be some—" he leans closer and lowers his voice "—smuggling going on. Have you heard any rumors?"

Ambar's eyes widen. "Smuggling? Like illegal arms and drugs?"

Joan wrinkles her nose. "We can't comment on what products might be involved, but it's definitely illegal. So, we're looking for any unusual behavior. Have you seen anything?"

Asking a new intern if they've noticed any unusual behavior among the other employees ought to set off alarms in Ambar's brain, but she doesn't hesitate. "People here spend a lot of time at the gym," she says.

"Ha! That's what I said!" I laugh.

Joan gives me the stink eye. "That's fairly common among ship crew. People get into a routine, and if you aren't dancing, you need some other form of physical activity."

The girl nods her dark head, impressed by this logic.

"We're more interested in relationships," Ty puts in. "People hanging around together who don't seem to have much in common. Whispered conversations. Arguments. Have you seen anything like that?"

Ambar opens her mouth to answer, then holds up a finger. "Hang on, call coming in. From Assistant Purser Watkins! Yes, ma'am?"

We listen to Ambar's side of the conversation, giving each other meaningful looks. After a few 'yes, ma'am' and 'no ma'am's, Ambar glares at me then signs off. "She said my cam is off!" Her eyes narrow.

O'Neill holds up a hand. "We can't have anyone listening to our discussions. Since we're investigating *them*."

"Oh, yeah." Ambar's face falls. "But I told her I'd get it turned back on. Maybe you should tell her what's going on."

"No!" All three of us say, louder than any of us had intended.

Joan lowers her voice. "It's an internal investigation. We don't know who is involved. Don't worry, when it's complete, your assistance will be noted in your personnel files. You might even get a commendation." She nods, wisely.

Ambar's eyes widen. "But what do I do? She asked me to turn my cam back on!"

"Don't worry, we're mostly done," Ty says soothingly. "If anyone asks, just tell them we were afraid someone might steal our choreography, and we were being extra careful. Triana will turn your cam back on, and you can go."

"But I don't want to go! This is exciting." Ambar's eyes start to water, as if she's going to cry. Again.

Joan puts a hand on the girl's shoulder. "I know it's exciting, but you have an important job to do for us, and we don't want you compromised. Keep looking for those odd interactions. If you notice anything, text me this code: Alturan timing sucks. Then I'll know you've got information for us, and we'll find a way to meet. In secret."

I reach up to rub my forehead, hopefully hiding the smirk on my face.

After the door shuts behind her, I reactivate her cam. I watch for a few seconds, to make sure she's really leaving. I set her cam to send a copy of the vid to my data pocket and check that her ring is on my watch list.

"That wasn't very helpful." Joan starts cleaning up our dinner.

Ty shrugs. "Better to know what she knows, and not have her spying on us. T, instead of tracking all these people, can you do another one of those data grabs and see who entered B-186?"

"It's already running." I swipe and flick. "I'm also checking the primary cargo hold entry. We should see a lot of movement there when docked and very little during transit. But I—" I pause for a second, setting some tricky filters. "I have it set to flag anyone unusual. Like that." I stare at the name that's popped up. "Look who visited the hold yesterday: Rael Ambani. Ser Skeevy."

CHAPTER TWENTY-FOUR

O'NEILL SITS up in his chair. "Did he go through B-186?"

I shake my head. "He went down the float tube, with Timmons."

"So maybe he's a customer, rather than an accomplice."

"Do you think Timmons was giving him a sales pitch?" Joan deepens her voice. "Why chase an intern when you can purchase your own human right here in my freezer."

"Ick." I pull up cam feeds. "I knew I should have put up my own cam down there. For some reason, this one doesn't have audio."

"I'm sure that's on purpose," O'Neill says. "Do you really think you'll find the vid? There are so many gaps in that surveillance feed it shouldn't even be called that anymore."

I throw the feed up on the mirror and fast forward, flicking from cam to cam as Skeevy and Timmons move. They walked through most of the hold but didn't stop to look at anything. "There don't appear to be any gaps! Do you think they just decided this would be a pleasant place for a stroll?"

O'Neill runs his hand through his perfect hair. "I don't know. Look, it's getting late. Joan has friends to meet. We don't want to make anyone suspicious. I think our best course of action is to just leave this alone. I'll contact the station to have security available when we dock, and they can sort out the details. If they can get to those people before Timmons can move them, they should be able to collect plenty of evidence."

I start to protest, but O'Neill cuts me off. "Don't forget—we're in inter-planetary space until tomorrow. If they find out we're on to them, they can space us and the only ones who would have authority to investigate would be security from the cruise line's planet of registry."

"Bermuda?" Joan says with horror. "Forget it—they believe the best form of investigation is a well-greased palm."

"Not to mention, we'd be dead," I mutter.

"There is that," O'Neill says. "I need to check in with DiFilippi. Joan, where are you off to?"

"Back to Taygete." She shrugs. "It's where most of the instructors hang out—and a few of the experienced passengers. Not glitzy enough for the first-timers, and that's how we like it."

O'Neill nods. "I'd recommend you stay in locations with plenty of people —non-crew if possible. And active cams. If they're onto us, we don't want it to be too easy for them to get rid of us."

"With five roommates meeting me at Taygete, I should be plenty safe. You two be careful, too."

"We'll walk together to the float tubes." He turns to me. "I need to check in with Sasha. Do you want to come, or shall I take you to my cabin first?"

"Your cabin?" I ask.

He leans in close and drops his voice so Joan can't hear. "You know my job is to keep you safe. You'd be safer there than in your own cabin." He's smart enough to make that sound like a suggestion instead of a command.

Joan opens the door, and we follow her out. At the float tube lobby, a boisterous group of passengers shout out her name. She smiles and waves. "I'll be fine with them. See you tomorrow!" She gives us a wink and disappears into the crowd.

"I'm tired, so I think I'll go to sleep." I really don't want to watch Ty and Sasha talk shop together. "Where are you meeting DiFilippi?"

"We don't have a meeting scheduled. I'm just going down to G Deck to see if she's in her office. If she isn't maybe I can get something out of Countryman. And I should be able to make a secure call to the station. But I'll take you up to my suite first."

"I can hook you up with a secure call," I step into the float tube with him.

"From my suite?"

I shake my head, sadly. "Do you really have to ask?"

He grins. "Good point. Let's do it."

We step out of the float tube on N Deck and head to the bow of the ship. As we round the first corner, a familiar voice calls out, "Hey! Tree!"

"What are you doing up here, TC?" I ask. "Aren't you still on duty?"

"Yeah." He looks around the deserted hall. "I'm stealing some chocolates from the stewards up here. Our deck is out."

"Why don't you just order more?" Ty asks.

"I don't know," TC wails. "There's some kind of war going on between the different decks. It's all about making points by stealing things. I'd rather just run down to supply, but Peters told me and Steve to get them from other decks. Steve's down on K, but those guys are ruthless. I hope he doesn't get caught."

I glance at his nametag, and step out of range, remembering the camera. "Is this for the show?" I point at my chest, where my nametag would be, if I wore one.

He shrugs and wipes his brow. "Probably. I'm not cut out for this. What are you two doing?

"I'm going to bed," I say. "He's going to make a call to his, uh, mother."

"Speaking of calls—" O'Neill gestures to his ring. I nod and he takes a couple steps away from TC. At least, I think it's TC's cam mic he's stepping away from, not my listening ears. A second later, he's back. "That was Sasha. She has some info for me. TC, would you walk Triana back to the Maia Suite? I can call my, uh, mother, later."

TC nods. "Can I swipe the chocolates on the way?"

"Sure, I'll help you." I give O'Neill a little finger wave and follow TC down the hall.

I keep lookout while TC slips into the steward's station and snags a bag of Pleiades Line chocolates. Then we scramble down the hall, and he lets us into the Maia Suite. I'm giggling by the time we get there, but TC looks a little green. "You feeling okay?" I ask.

He grimaces. "I, yeah, I'm fine." He looks around the room, as if he's never seen it before. "Listen, I need your help."

"Sure." I drop onto the couch. "What's the problem?"

"Remember when we were down in—" I hold up a finger and he breaks off.

Flicking through my holo-screens, I activate a scramble field within the suite. "I don't want your nametag recording anything inconvenient."

TC grunts. "Thanks. I can't take it off during my shift, but it's not my fault if a passenger jams it. Of course, you aren't really a passenger."

"No, but I'm a guest of a passenger, and we're in a passenger's suite, which should be safe from Big Brother."

"Who?" TC asks.

"Big Brother. Observation. Oversight." I shake my head. "Doesn't matter. What's up?"

He opens and closes his mouth a couple times. He definitely looks ill. Finally, he speaks in a rush. "I think I left something down in that cabin. B-186. I dropped my nametag somewhere, and I'm pretty sure it was there. This is a replacement."

I stare at him. "And you're waiting until now to tell me? How did you get a replacement?"

He looks away. "I borrowed it from Arstend. He's working days. See?" He leans forward so I can see the paper peeling away from the plastek tag. "I just stuck my name over his."

"But what about the cams? Haven't they noticed you're showing up on the wrong feed?"

Another pause. Then, "I hacked it."

Of course, he did. It's exactly what I would have done. "Well, I guess we'd better get down there and retrieve the evidence, right?"

While TC hacks back into Arstend's nametag cam and sets up a vid loop, I start to do the same for the cams on the corridor outside B-186. Except someone else has already set this up. I glance at TC.

"This might not be the best time to do this. It looks like someone might be in there already. I'm going to run a data grab to see if anyone has been down there tonight." I flick open a new screen on my holo-ring.

TC blanches. "Then we need to go now. If they're down there, they might find it."

"We can't just blunder into the room if someone is in there!" I set up my grab and start it running.

TC heads for the door. "No one will be in the cabin! They'll be down in the hold."

I follow him down the corridor at a run, dodging curious passengers. I catch up to him in the lobby, but before I can reply, he steps into the float tube and zips down. I heave a sigh and follow him.

Jumping out of the tube, I lunge forward and grab TC's arm. "We don't know who's in there, or when they went in. We could easily run into them on their way up or down the ladder. And besides, how do you know you lost the nametag in that cabin? Maybe it's down in the hold."

He shakes me off and jogs away. "I checked the location—it's definitely in the cabin." He throws the statement over his shoulder as he dashes between two crew members strolling down the corridor toward us.

I smile at them and shrug, then bolt after him, hissing, "Ix-nay on the abin-cay."

"What?" He stops long enough to give me a blank stare, then plunges on.

"It's *Ancient TēVē* slang for 'shut up, that's classified'." We dash around another corridor and through the holographic "closed" sign that hovers across the passageway. "Zark! I hope that sign doesn't have an alert attached to it."

"It didn't give us away last time." TC keeps running.

"It wasn't here last time." I slow to a walk. "Something's not right. Why wasn't it here last time?"

"Come on!" TC stops in front of the cabin door. "My badge cam doesn't show anyone inside, so let's get this done."

"TC, something isn't right," I repeat, stopping beside him.

"What does your data grab show?" His voice is shaky and sweat beads on his forehead. We didn't run that hard.

I check my results. "Nothing. No one has been down here all evening."

"Great." He doesn't sound great.

"Are you okay?"

"I'll be fine when we get this done." He flashes a nervous look at me. With a flick of his holo, the door slides open.

"Maybe I should stay out here. To keep watch—since the hall cams are down." I take a half-step away from the door.

TC grabs my arm and drags me into the cabin. "No! I need you inside!" The door slides shut behind us.

And Sasha DiFilippi steps out of the tiny bathroom.

CHAPTER TWENTY-FIVE

"I THOUGHT you were meeting O'Neill in your office." I glare at DiFilippi. "Is he here, too?"

"No." The security agent looks me up and down. "He's meeting with Officer Countryman. They're working on a plan to notify the station of the illegal activities occurring on this ship."

I nod. "You aren't worried about tipping off the bad guys? Although, I guess if security is waiting when we dock, they can't really escape, right?"

She smiles. She looks different today—harder somehow. "We aren't worried about them escaping. Thanks for bringing her down, TC."'

I look at TC. The sheen on his face makes him look feverish. "Did you know she was down here? I thought you said the cabin was empty."

TC swallows, hard. "She asked me to bring you here, without telling you why."

"What?" I turn back to DiFilippi. "Why didn't you just call me? I'd have come down."

The woman strolls behind me, and I turn to keep her in sight. She's kinda giving me the creeps.

"I didn't want you mentioning our meeting to Agent O'Neill." She gestures to the bunk. "I'd like you to accompany me to the cargo hold, please." She turns to TC. "You're dismissed."

TC hesitates.

"Now." DiFilippi doesn't raise her voice, but TC's eyes grow wider, and he steps back toward the door.

"You're going to let Sandrine go, aren't you?" His voice cracks on the girl's name.

"Of course." DiFilippi smiles. "She'll be in the Taygete Lounge in a few minutes. Why don't you go find her?"

"What's going on?" I ask. "What does Sandrine have to do with this?"

DiFilippi leans into the bunk and lifts the panel. "Don't worry about it. TC and I have a little arrangement."

TC takes one last look at me and bolts out the door. It swishes shut behind him.

I narrow my eyes at DiFilippi. "What's going on?" I repeat, leaning back against the bulkhead, crossing my arms over my chest, pretending to be all casual. In reality, my heartbeat sounds like a snare drum in my ears. "Why do you want to go down there? And what did TC mean about letting Sandrine go?"

DiFilippi pulls a weapon from her belt and aims it at me. "I want you to go down there because I intend to add you to our frozen stockpile of inconvenient nuisances. We're going to use you as collateral to make sure Agent O'Neill doesn't cause any problems by contacting his friends on the station. And then we're going to sell you to the highest bidder."

The light in my brain finally flashes on. "You're the one who put Les in the freezer!"

She rolls her eyes. "Took you long enough to figure that out. Now, downstairs, please, or I'll have to shoot you first. Just makes it harder for all of us. You don't look like a lightweight, and I'd hate to drop your unconscious body down there." She points through the bunk down at the cargo hold. "It's a long way down. Might hurt."

"Now wait just a minute! What makes you say I don't look like a lightweight? I'm pretty sure I weigh less than you!"

She gives her head a little shake, as if she can't believe what I just said. "Just get down there!" She makes a menacing movement with the weapon.

I peer at the gun. I'm pretty sure she won't kill me outright, but I'm not positive. "I don't think putting me in your freezer is a good move. Ty will come looking for me." I glance through the opening in the bunk without leaving my position by the door. The ladder stretches down into the dark hold. Even though I know what's down there, I don't want to go. Or maybe, especially since I know what's down there.

DiFilippi growls—an actual animal sound. She jerks the weapon again, and I take a tiny step toward the bunk. My mind races, trying to come up with an escape plan. Maybe if I stall long enough, TC will get help.

"What did TC mean about Sandrine?" I ask, taking another tiny step forward, just to stop her growling.

"We threatened to throw her in the freezer if he didn't help us. He's so gullible." She laughs harshly.

"So, she's not down there?" I slide another half-step closer to the bunk.

"Why don't you go down and find out." DiFilippi grasps my arm and yanks.

Big mistake. On her part.

My self-defense training kicks in, and my reflexes take over. With a lighting twist of my hand against her thumb, I break her grip. Then, in a move worthy of Joan's choreography, I grab her wrist and lift my arm, spinning underneath. I end up behind her, with her arm twisted up against her back. Then I fling my other arm around her neck and pull my inner elbow against her throat, choking her.

Sasha struggles for a moment then flings her head back and slams it into my face. Pain explodes through my nose, cheeks, and head. I shove her away, hard. "You *ceiling fan*!" Tears stream from my eyes. "You broke my nose!" I blindly swipe at my face, holding up my other hand in a sad attempt to keep her away.

"You got some skills, girl," a voice says behind me.

I spin around, smearing tears and blood across my cheeks. Standing in front of the closing door, Joan waves and smiles. Sasha is nowhere to be seen. Joan points to the bunk. I stumble over and look down. The lights have come on in the cargo hold. Beneath us, Sasha DiFilippi lies on the top crate, out cold.

"Did I do that?" I stare down at the crumpled security agent.

Joan chuckles. "You had a little help." She holds out a plastek straw.

I stare at her hand. "You helped me by having a margarita?"

"I had to drink the margarita to get the straw. But then I used it with one of these." She stretches out her other hand and shows me one of those frilled toothpicks that delis stick in your sandwich, pinched carefully between her thumb and forefinger.

"You shot DiFilippi with a decorative food pick." I give her a look. "Did she trip into the bunk while swatting it away?"

"No, I think the tranquilizer I dipped it into might have had something to do with her current location. Although, you almost got her in there without me. That was a pretty accurate shove for someone who just took a head butt."

"Total coincidence. I was just trying to get away from her rock-hard skull." I swipe at my face again, but the bleeding seems to have stopped. "What are you doing here, anyway? Please don't tell me you're in this with DiFilippi, too. I liked you!"

Joan waves her hands, boneless arms flying. "No, no. TC contacted me after he left you here. He said something about you needing backup. I came in just as you twisted DiFilippi's arm up behind her. Didn't you hear me yell?" She turns and waves the door open.

"No, what did you yell?" I follow her out the door.

"Watch out for the headbutt."

I laugh. "Thanks."

"Don't mention it. Listen, I tried to contact Ty, but he's not answering." She trots away up the corridor toward the float tubes. "Do you know where he is?"

"He was supposed to meet Sasha in the security office. I think Countryman is up there. Sasha was planning on using me to coerce him into letting the whole slavery thing slide. Like that would work." I stop next to her at the float tube, breathing heavily already. "Maybe I *should* start going to the gym."

Joan turns and looks at me. "Somehow I think that might have backfired on them. The coercion, not the gym thing. You should definitely join my Cross-Pump class. In the meantime, let's get you cleaned up."

We take the float tube down to the costume closet near Joan's room. While she picks out an outfit for me, I take a minute to clean the blood off my face. Luckily, my nose isn't broken—surprisingly, it looks fine once I wash it.

When I emerge from the lav, she hands me a hangar and a wig. "Put these on. I'm going brunette, you'll be blonde. That should help us hide from anyone looking for us."

We put on the dance costumes—pretty, but not too flashy. The blonde wig and tiny hat with a sequined veil should throw off any casual observers and might even fool the facial recognition software. Joan wears long dark brown tresses and a flowing gold gown.

We take the float tube up to G Deck. Joan starts toward the Security office, but I grab her arm. "Are you sure this is a good idea? We're sitting ducks until we reach Crippen-Hauck. They can do whatever they want to us."

Joan raises her eyebrows. "Maybe if you tell them who you are, they'll realize that's not a good idea. I assume they're trying to stay under the radar."

"What do you mean?" I try to sound casual, but my breathing speeds up.

"Kidnapping the daughter of the CEO is not a good way to keep your slavery ring in the shadows." She grins at my expression. "Don't worry, I don't think anyone else knows."

"How'd you figure it out?" I think back through our conversations, but I can't remember saying anything that might have tipped her off.

"I've seen your picture. And I thought it was odd that a board security agent was travelling solo in the best suite on the ship. But why are you on the payroll?" She leads the way into the diner where we ate—was it only two nights ago?

I explain about my job on the station, and my desire to stay incognito. "I don't have any vacation time, so I had to accept a transfer."

Joan laughs so hard tears roll down her face. "You are the weirdest heiress I've ever met."

"Have you met a lot of them?" I take a seat at the bar and start to order a bottle of water then stop. "Maybe we shouldn't order anything—they'll be able to track our purchases."

"As you demonstrated earlier, they can track us anyway. Unless you use one of these." She hands me a small silver envelope.

"That looks like the thing TC keeps his nametag in when he's off duty." I finger the slippery fabric. "It blocks holo-ring signals?"

Joan nods, adding another water to the order and swiping the charge-to-room icon. Then she pulls her ring off and slides it into another silver envelope. "They know we're here, now. Put your ring inside that thing, and let's make ourselves scarce."

CHAPTER TWENTY-SIX

WE GRAB our beverages and slip out the door, waving off the hostess who appears at the entrance. "Sorry, we decided we're not hungry yet." My face feels stiff, but the smile seems to convince the woman. We stroll toward the float tubes and waft up to the StarDeck. "Where are we going to hide?"

"To use a cliché, right here in plain sight." Joan weaves through the throngs of passengers and takes a seat at a small table near the door to the kitchen. "Alternate exit." She nods at the kitchen door. "Screened, but clear line of sight to the entrance." She tips her head at the hydroponic plants behind me. "Large crowd to hide in. Now, we need to figure out what we're going to do until we arrive at Crippen-Hauck."

"I'm going to start by sending a message to Ty." I lift my hand then realize my ring is stowed away in the silver envelope in my pocket. 'Well, zark! How am I going to contact him?"

Joan laughs. "You haven't spent much time on a luxury cruise ship, have you?"

"I used to travel with Mother—"

"But not as an adult. These ships are set up to allow all kinds of anonymous hookups." She pokes at the table. In seconds, she's pulled up a dating app. With a couple swipes, O'Neill's face appears with a passenger number beneath. "We can send him an anonymous message here. We need to come up with something he'll know came from you. Do you two have any private jokes?"

"If I told you, I'd have to shoot you." I give a sickly smirk. "Let me think for a minute. What do we want to tell him? Where we are, of course. We probably don't want to mention anyone else, but we need to make sure he knows that they know we know. Oh! I've got it."

I reach across the table, swipe the app to me and type:

Meet me in the Grendel's lair

Don't psych yourself out.

Carrots or fries?

I slide the app back to Joan. "Cryptic enough?"

"I have no idea what you're talking about, so it's perfect." Joan hits send. "I assume Ty will understand?"

I smile. "We met Lady Grandelle here the first night out, and he knows I call her the Grendel. The second line refers to an *Ancient TēVē* series we binged last week. The theme song says something about 'I know, you know, they know.' And carrots or fries is just to confirm it's me."

She sits back and lifts her water bottle in toast. "Works for me. I'll watch to see if anyone follows him in. Can we do anything about the cams in here? I'm sure they'll keep an eye on him."

I start to flick my ring again. "Zark! No ring. This is hard. There's nothing I can do about the cams without access to the OS. Is there someplace we could meet that isn't under surveillance?"

"Didn't you divert the feed from my cabin? We could meet there. Although somewhere completely unrelated to any of us would be better." Joan leans forward. "Probably the safest place would be in the cargo hold. They'd never expect that."

I shake my head. "Not going there. They may want to put us on ice, but I'm not going to make it easy for them. Plus, Sasha is down there. Hey, you said TC contacted you. Where is he?"

She shrugs. "Down in Taygete, checking up on his girlfriend."

"And she's probably chatting up Ser Skeevy, who might be in on this whole thing." I start to shove my fingers through my hair and remember the wig. "Okay, we have to stay safe for about twenty-four more hours—the ship docks at midnight tomorrow." I pick at the label on my water bottle.

"We'll need to find somewhere safe to hide until then. We can't hang out in here forever. We'll need to sleep sometime."

Joan jerks her chin at a drunk snoring in the next booth. "Apparently, we can sleep here." She laughs. "I suppose we could just barricade ourselves inside Ty's suite. There's plenty of room. Are Countryman and DiFilippi going to break in and arrest us?"

"They aren't going to arrest us," I correct her. "They're going to freeze us. We'll just disappear, like Les."

"And your mother will launch a full investigation. I still think leaking your identity is the safest thing we could do."

I shake my head. "Human trafficking is bad. If I had a choice of freezing an heiress or going to trial for slavery, I know which one I'd choose. By the time my mother found out I was missing, they'd be long gone. No, first we need to make sure O'Neill contacts the station. I'm sure Countryman was supposed to stop him from doing that. Then we need to find a place to hide until we get there."

A voice booms out through the room. "It's time for the crew dance-off, where members of the crew compete for bragging rights and time off! Let's give a warm StarDeck welcome to our first couple, Random and Kindra!"

What the heck? "They're supposed to be on duty!" I'm so mad, I'm spitting.

"That means Ops is empty," Joan says. "Maybe you can sneak in and find us a place to hide."

Oh, yeah, I don't care if they aren't working, right? Not my circus, not my monkeys. I start to rise from my chair, but a hand on my shoulder presses me back down.

With a yelp, I turn, to find O'Neill perching on the arm of my chair. I throw my arms around him and press my face into his abs. His hard, muscular abs.

He strokes my back and kisses my wig. "Ew, this hair is really stiff."

Laughter bubbles up inside me. Just being near him makes everything better. I feel like a walking rom-com cliché.

"How'd you recognize me?" I loosen my death grip around his waist and adjust the wig.

"I'd know you anywhere," he says. "Plus, I knew Joan has mad Marine skills, so I asked myself where a professional would hide in this room. Behind the plants by the kitchen door, of course."

Joan gives him a little head-nod of acknowledgement.

O'Neill steps away to drag an empty chair up to the table. "So, what's going on?"

I groan. "It would take hours to tell you all that! I was really hoping you'd know."

Joan takes a deep breath. "Countryman and DiFilippi are involved, so we'll get no help from them. They know we found the cargo in the freezer. Ollie's involvement is still unconfirmed. Ops is empty right now." Joan tips her head toward the dance floor where Kindra and Random whirl through a series of turns and spins. "Have you called the station yet?"

Maybe not hours.

Behind me, the kitchen door slides open, and Joan gasps.

O'Neill and I turn to look.

Speak of the devil. Countryman stands in the opening.

CHAPTER TWENTY-SEVEN

"ZARK!" I holler.

O'Neill says something else, a bit stronger.

"Quick, onto the floor!" Joan leaps to her feet and yanks us toward the dance floor.

"What?! No!" I hang back, digging in my heels.

O'Neill and Joan make eye contact, and O'Neill nods. "Now, Triana. No arguments." He pulls me to my feet and drags me between the tables to the empty space. Joan, a few meters ahead of us, darts out onto the floor. When Random spins Kindra out for a few solo steps, Joan cuts in and grabs Random's hand. Kindra turns, hand extended to Random, but Joan puts out her other hand and swings her in. The crowd goes wild.

"Ladies and gentlemen, you never know what's going to happen on crew night, but this is new, even for me!" The announcer laughs. He stands near the musicians in front of the wide windows across the bow of the ship. Starlight glints off his sparkling silver suit as he raises his arm to gesture to the dancers. "Let's give a warm welcome to our third dancer, Joan Lesley! Joan has a string of professional dance titles longer than my arm, including Galactic Pro Champion for three years running! Joan Lesley!" He applauds loudly, encouraging the crowd to emulate his example.

Ty pulls me close and twirls us out onto the edge of the floor on the far side from the announcer. "The dance show cams are live." He nods at the red-lighted drones hovering quietly above the edges of the floor. "The show is broadcast live to S'Ride and Crippen-Hauck, so they can't lay a finger on us without millions of witnesses. What's Countryman doing?"

I glance back to the kitchen. "He's waving at someone. Near the door."

Countryman has stalked into the room and is waving at someone near the entrance. Ty turns me across the edge of the dance floor, and DiFilippi spins into view. She looks terrible. Her hair is a mess, and she limps as she walks. A huge, red welt covers her forehead, and one eye is swollen and rapidly turning black.

"Wow, what happened to her?"

I smile in satisfaction. "Me and Joan."

He looks down at me. "And not a scratch on you."

I shrug. "Had a bloody nose earlier. But Joan's really good with a blow dart."

"I'm not even going to ask."

"Look at that footwork!" The announcer's voice cuts through the music. "Joan sure knows how to lead! That's what I call a champion, folks!"

In the middle of the floor, Joan spins Kindra one way and Random the other, leading them past each other like a well synchronized machine. Random follows her lead as if they've been partners for years, hamming it up for the audience. Joan grins, clearly having the time of her life. Even Kindra is smiling.

Suddenly, the announcer notices us on the edge of the floor. "What's this, friends? A new couple trying to steal the limelight? And one of them is a passenger!" The announcer flicks his holo-ring and leans toward the bartender. "We have a mystery entry! Show us what you've got, folks!"

A spotlight stabs down at us. O'Neill smiles and I swear I hear women sigh. "Ready?" he asks me.

"For what?" I yelp.

"Just follow my lead." And with that, he amps up the smile another hundred watts and spins me out into the center of the floor. With light but firm pressure on my back, he guides me into the opening sequence of his and Ambar's routine. I watched them practice it so many times, I've almost got it memorized. But Ty is such an amazing leader, I could have done most of it without any preparation. Adrenaline pumps through my body, and I feel like I've been sprinkled with pixie dust.

We soar around the dance floor, spinning, turning, kicking, and jumping. Our feet move like clockwork, and we prance through the Alturan timing like pros. Why did I think performing would be so arduous? This is amazing! My heart pounds in time to the music.

"Incoming!" O'Neill whispers right before he spins me out to arm's length. In the brief pause at the end of his fingertips, I see Countryman headed my direction. I spin back in and duck under Ty's kick. Popping back up, I jump over his leg and turn to find DiFilippi stalking in from the opposite side.

"What do we do?" I cry when he pulls me back into closed position. I glance over at Joan, but she's disappeared, and Random and Kindra are continuing on alone. They don't look as polished without her. "Where's Joan?"

"Over there!" O'Neill turns us until I'm facing the band. Joan stands beside the announcer, talking at lightning speed, her arms waving, hands gesturing. She points at the furious security agents closing in on the dance floor. The announcer shakes his head, holding up his hands as if trying to stop Joan's disclosures.

"What's she saying?" I ask.

O'Neill shakes his head. "Whatever it is, it doesn't seem to be helping." He steers me toward the bow of the ship, away from agents. "When we get to the side, run!" On the word, we reach the edge of the dance floor and he leaps into the narrow space between tables, dragging me after him.

We dodge around drunk passengers, leaping over legs lounging across the aisles. I crash into a waitress with a full tray of drinks, sending slushy iced cocktails all over her and the patrons behind her. O'Neill doesn't even slow down. "Sorry!" I cry over my shoulder.

He whips me around a decorative room divider, and we're assaulted by the overwhelming smell of fried food. We scramble through a throng of flower-shirted partiers. We dive under a limbo bar and slide across the slippery, shining floor. O'Neill pops upright again and yanks me up with him. "This way!"

We race past a heavily laden buffet and slam into a huge man with a towering plate. The man bounces back, his plate sailing up into the air. Before he can even open his mouth to yell, O'Neill snags the plate. Lightning fast, he catches the massive pile of food as it falls, setting the plate gently on the table next to him. One lonely chocolate dipped strawberry teeters on the edge of the plate then tumbles toward the floor. I lunge forward and grab it out of the air before it hits the ground. Then we're off again.

I feel like a kite that's been tied to a speed bubble on Diamond Beach during the afternoon gales. Dragging against the pull, but helpless to slow it down.

We swerve around a gaggle of elderly women, giggling together over something. I do a double-take. With the widespread availability of regenerative medicine, you don't often see obviously old people. Especially not in the demographic that can afford a cruise. Then I notice the matching T-shirts with the New Hallelujah logo. These women must be members of the Church of Nature, taking their end-of-life walk-about. The faithful take a year off during their eighth decade—if they survive that long—to cut loose before their bodies wear out. The women smile and wave as we pelt past.

O'Neill yanks me around a corner, and we duck behind a wall of potted plants. I gasp for air, my lungs heaving.

"Come on," he whispers, his breathing even and slow.

I really need to hit the gym.

We creep behind the plants back toward the dance floor of the massive StarDeck. The band continues to play, and Random and Kindra dance on. The announcer and Countryman stand by the band, clearly arguing. Countryman holds Joan by the wrist, while she stands quietly.

My eyes dart around the room, looking for Sasha. A shriek from behind the divider—probably the New Hallelujah ladies from the sound—echoes across the room. "That's got to be her," I tell O'Neill.

He gives me a quick glance, then makes a face at Joan. She winks back at us and reaches slowly into her pocket.

"Come on, let's see if we can get to the door." O'Neill straightens up and crooks his elbow. I slide my hand onto his arm, and we merge into the crowd swirling around the outer reaches of the room. Trying to look casual, I nibble at my purloined strawberry. It is excellent.

Out on the dance floor, the music flourishes and ends. Kindra and Random take a bow in the center of the lighted space. The announcer is so busy arguing with Countryman, he doesn't notice the dance has ended. The bartender leans over and hisses something at him, and the announcer jerks. He makes some choppy gestures at Countryman and swings back to the audience, a huge smile plastered on his face.

"Let's hear some love for Kindra and Random!" The crowd applauds. Then he reaches back to take Joan's hand, leading her forward and away from Countryman. "And for the amazing Joan Lesley!" The spotlight swings away from the floor and shines down on Joan. She smiles and waves. The crowd goes wild.

Unnoticed in the dark behind the spot-lit dais, Countryman sinks to the floor like a pile of sand dumped from a bucket. I stare, like a yokel from Armstrong. Joan must have had another dart up her sleeve.

Next to me, O'Neill slams to a halt. I turn in alarm. He stands nose to nose with Sasha. "Agent DiFilippi," he says with a nod. "You don't look well today. Maybe you should sit down and rest."

Sasha growls.

Ty bares his teeth in a menacing grin.

On the far edge of the dance floor, Kindra stares in my direction. Our eyes meet and she raises an eyebrow. What does she want?

After a second, her eyes dart away and back to me. The second time she does it, I turn to see what she's looking at. Then I make eye contact again and smile. Kindra nods once and flicks her holo-ring.

"You two need to come with me," Sasha says, eyes narrow.

"I don't think so," O'Neill says pleasantly. "I have no desire to end up in your freezer."

"I wouldn't waste a freezer case on you."

"You sound like a bad *Ancient TēVē* vid." Watching Kindra out of the corner of my eye, I start edging away from Sasha, gripping O'Neill's arm so he has to move with me.

"You *will* shut up," Sasha says. "And the two of you will proceed to the door in an orderly fashion. If you don't, I will shoot you both and claim you were terrorists."

"That's not going to stand up to any scrutiny," O'Neill says in the same even voice. He glances at me and shifts his weight in my direction.

"It doesn't have to stand up to scrutiny." Sasha smirks. "It just has to stand up until I get off this tub."

A siren blares out. Lights flash. The sound of thousands of coins thundering to the floor rings through the room.

"Run!" I scream.

Hundreds of hollering passengers descend on the doors to the lobby. DiFilippi fights the crowd but gets dragged along in the relentless flow. I pull O'Neill the other direction, aiming for the kitchen.

"Another jackpot!" The announcer screams over the cacophony.

CHAPTER TWENTY-EIGHT

ANOTHER DELUGE of passengers flows onto the dance floor, led by the New Hallelujah ladies. They rush past us, bumping into tables, turning over chairs as they surge forward. I grab O'Neill's hand and drag him to the kitchen where we slam through the doors. The kitchen staff looks up in alarm.

"Don't mind us!" I say to the room at large, darting between the white coated staff. "Just escaping the bad guys." I give a little wave to Julian, the cheese aficionado I met at the crew party.

"Bad guys?" He brandishes his cleaver. "Need any help?"

I skid to a stop. "I don't want to get you in trouble. But if Agent DiFilippi shows up, could you slow her down? Accidentally, of course."

"DiFilippi? From the security office?" Julian grins. "We hate that *knife sharpener*. She takes a cut of any contraband we smuggle aboard. And she doesn't appreciate good cheese."

"Awesome! How do we get out of here without going through the StarDeck?"

Julian points at a door on the back wall labelled *Exit*. I give myself a dramatic palm-to-forehead slap and drag O'Neill away.

"Where's that leftover soup?" Julian calls as we pelt through the door. "The greasy garlic and pepper stuff?"

The exit leads to a back corridor, almost identical to any crew access on SK2. I stop and pull my holo-ring out of my pocket. I weigh the small silver packet in my palm, looking at O'Neill. "What do you think? Is it worth the risk?"

"I don't think anything is worth stopping right now." He points over his shoulder. "We need to move. As soon as she comes through that door, she's going to see us."

"Good point. Let's get a little more distance." I think for a second, imagining a mental schematic of the cruiser. "This way will take us to the cargo tubes. Then we can go anywhere in the ship."

O'Neill nods and takes off down the hall. I heave a sigh and follow. If my life is going to include this much running, I really should start working out.

We ignore the doors scattered along the hallway and run flat out for the end. There, the corridor jogs to the right and back to the left, hiding us from anyone emerging from the kitchen. I slow down a little, but O'Neill grabs my arm and pulls me along.

"You can rest in the float tube."

We arrive at the cargo tube few minutes later. I bend over, clutching the stitch in my side. O'Neill grimaces at me but doesn't say anything. He hands me a bottle of water—where has he been keeping it? Before I get my breathing under control to take a swig, he grabs me by the waist and lifts me into the tube with him. We free fall for a fraction of a second—I hate that part of the cargo tubes. Efficiency over comfort. Then the anti-grav catches us, and we speed down into the lower decks of the ship.

O'Neill shoves me out on I Deck. "Let's go to that spa where I used the med pod. It had multiple exits."

"How are we going to get in?" I ask after swallowing a gulp of water. "I could get us through the crew entrance, but that would tip off anyone looking for us. And that reminds me, you should give me your holo-ring. They can track you with that."

Ty slips his ring off and hands it to me. "If they're open late, we can just walk in as customers."

"They weren't open the other night." I follow him down the passageway.

"Yeah, I know." We round a corner, and a utility cart blocks the way. A pudgy boy with a rumpled uniform and acne peeks out of the open stateroom.

"Sorry, ser, sera. Let me move that cart." He hurries into the hall and pushes the cart against the wall.

"Steve! Remember me? From SK2?" I turn to O'Neill. "Steve here is one of the interns from the Techno-Inst. He beat Ambar at the centerpiece competition."

Ty reaches out a fist. "I've heard a lot about you, Steve."

"Really?" He timidly bumps fists with Ty. "Uh, I haven't heard anything about you."

"I'm sure you have," I say. "He's Ambar's dance partner."

"Oh. Yeah, I've heard way too much about you." Steve's face flushes. "Oh, sorry, that came out wrong."

O'Neill waves it away. "Don't worry about it. Listen, we have a problem, and you may be just the guy to help us."

I give O'Neill my best, are-you-sure-this-is-a-good-idea look, but he's totally focused on Steve. "We've run into a little snag. I broke up with my girlfriend yesterday, and I need a place to lay low. Can't stay in that tiny stateroom with her, you know?" He gives Steve a look that clearly says, "You and I are men of the galaxy who understand that women are crazy."

I roll my eyes, but Steve eats it up. "Yeah, I hear you. Well, there's an empty cabin down on G Deck. I can let you in, if you need a place to hide. But why don't you just hang in Triana's cabin?"

Ty leans in close and lowers his voice. "She has, like, twenty roommates. And we'd like some alone time, if you know what I mean."

He practically winks and nudges Steve. Seriously, I can't believe the kid is buying this.

But Steve grins like a puppy watching his master holding a piece of bacon. And gives a huge stage wink. "I can fix you up."

"Excellent. I owe you one, man. Is there a way to do this anonymously? The ex still has access to my holo-ring locator, and I'm afraid if I turn it off, she'll come unhinged."

Steve winks again and flicks his holo-ring. "Cabin G-43. I'll set the door to unlock in five minutes. It'll only stay that way for two minutes, though, so you'd better be ready. Oh, and the stairs are that way, if you want to avoid the float tubes." He points back over his shoulder, in the direction we were already going.

O'Neill slaps him on the back in a manly show of camaraderie and heads down the hall.

"Thanks, Steve." I charge after O'Neill.

The door marked Stairs opens on a dark well. As we step through, lights spring on. Thick carpeting covers the steps. Synth-wood wainscoting topped with floral print in the familiar, sickening peach, lime, and maroon, covers the walls. The scent of fresh-cut oranges fills the space. "Just two flights down." O'Neill points. "Have you gotten your second wind?"

"Yeah, I'm fine," I grumble. "In general, we spend way too much time in stairwells, don't you think? Why can't we ever make our escape through a massage pod? Or a hot tub?"

"That was a terrible vid." He rounds the corner on the first landing and continues down. "Don't worry, you'll have time to rest when we get to G-43."

"Are you sure we should trust Steve? I mean, anyone who can make Ambar cry is, well—anyone can make Ambar cry, so that isn't a good recommendation."

He laughs. "He's an intern. He's not likely to have connections among the underworld of the ship."

"Yeah, that's what I thought about TC, and he turned me in to DiFilippi. I thought we were friends."

"What?" O'Neill stops on the H Deck landing. "Seriously?"

"Yeah, your new partner blackmailed him into luring me down to B Deck. She threatened to throw Sandrine into the freezer. But it's okay, he sent Joan to rescue me." I swing around the corner and start down to G Deck.

"Hang on." O'Neill doesn't move. "Maybe we shouldn't trust Steve. Sasha knows you all embarked together on SK2. She might think you two are friends and use that. We didn't tell him not to talk to security."

"I'm so tired of thinking about all the possibilities. Can't we just find somewhere to hide? We just have to stay hidden until we make Crippen-Hauck. Oh, and you need to call your buddies over there, to have security waiting for us when we arrive." I rub my face. "No need to make it secure—

we've been busted. You can do that from Steve's cabin—unless they've blocked all off-ship calls. I don't know if they can even do that."

"Let's go find out." He sighs and follows me down to G. When the door slides open, he goes into secret agent mode, and ducks around the door jamb to take a quick look into the hall. "Clear."

I shake my head and follow him out. At this point, I'd almost be happy to get captured, because it would mean I could stop moving.

"Let's make the call, then move again, just in case," O'Neill says when we reach G-43 and find the door open as promised. He steps across the tiny cabin to the communications console, while I make use of the facilities.

"I'm sending you a full data dump right now," O'Neill is saying to an invisible colleague when I emerge from the bathroom. He turns to me. "Can you download all that vid data you've been hiding away?"

I step into pickup range. "I can send you everything, but it's a *pillow*-ton of raw footage. Most of it will be useless. And it will take forever to transmit."

"That's okay," a familiar voice says over the comms. "Just start transmitting. Anything you've got. We've got the computing power to filter through it all. The more you can send us, the more leverage you'll have if you get taken."

I hit the mute button. "Is that Vanti?"

"Yeah. She was detailed to S'Ride after we finished on Kaku. We're talking directly to the planet, but she will have Crippen-Hauck security waiting when we arrive on station." He slaps the mute off. "We'll get it started. Just make sure you pick up those people we identified—especially DiFilippi and Countryman—and don't let any crew depart the terminal until you've had a chance to clear them."

"Don't tell me how to do my job, Griz," Vanti says, dryly. "Keep safe. And, Triana, get that data stream started."

"Yes, ma'am." I snap a jaunty salute that she can't see. "Let's go down to Ops. Kindra helped us with the slot machines, so maybe she'll help us again."

"That was her?" O'Neill waves open the door and does his secret agent routine again. Satisfied, he moves to the stairwell for a repeat performance.

"It was her trick, and she tipped me a nod just before they paid out." I trot down the first set of steps and stop at a door labeled *Crew Members*

Only. With a shrug, I pull my holo-ring out of my pocket and slide it out of the foil envelope. "We're on the clock, now. If they're looking, they'll find us."

"But it takes a while," O'Neill says, hopefully. "I mean, they have the whole ship to search. It took hours for you to get ring data on Ollie."

"Yeah, but I was searching a much longer time-frame." I palm the ID panel and the heavy hatch opens. We run through, barreling down the steps. On the crew side, the stairwell goes from cozy wood-paneling and carpeted treads to utilitarian metal steps and pipe-style railing. "They only have to find us *now*."

As we thunder down the hollow-sounding steps, I slide the ring back into the packet. "But as long as I keep this thing in the envelope, they have to actually be looking at the moment I pull it out. Ten seconds ago, I showed up. Now, I'm gone." I wave the silver envelope triumphantly, and it slips out of my fingers.

I lunge forward, tripping down the next two steps as I try to catch the slippery, silver packet. I fumble it off the tips of my fingers. Twice. Then I slam into the landing wall. And the packet falls between the railings, tumbling down the long stairwell, bouncing off the walls and treads.

Tink.

Tink.

Tink.

CHAPTER TWENTY-NINE

"THAT WAS BOTH OUR RINGS, wasn't it?" O'Neill asks as we pound down the next flight of stairs.

"Yes," I whisper. "But the good news is, we have to go all the way to B Deck anyway. We just have to make sure we don't run past it on the way."

"True enough." I can't tell if he's humoring me, or really agreeing. Not that it matters. "I just hope neither of them fell out on the way down."

I shake my head. "It was closed."

"Well, that's something."

Four flights later, I'm exhausted. I stumble down the last few steps to find O'Neill standing in the center of the stairwell, holding the tiny metallic envelope in his palm. He gazes up the stairwell. "Good thing holo-rings are sturdy." His lips twitch as he hands me the packet.

I have a bit of a history with holo-ring disasters.

But when I open the packet, the rings appear to be fine. I slide mine onto my finger and wave my hand at the stairwell door. Nothing happens. I give O'Neill a weak grin and try again.

Nothing.

I flick my ring, and it lights up. "It seems to be working fine. I can access my messages. Look here's one from Joan. It just says, 'Where are you?'"

O'Neill wraps his warm hand around mine. "Don't answer. We don't know who can read that."

A thick panel slides out of the deck above us and slams across the top of the flight of stairs, creating an impenetrable ceiling in the middle of the stairwell. "That's the decompression bulkhead," I say, trying for nonchalant. My voice quavers. "Either the ship's been hit by a meteor, or they've found us."

The heavy hatch behind us grinds open. We both spin around, dropping into a fighting stance. Well, O'Neill drops into a fighting stance. I just crouch down and hope for the best. Surprise was on my side last time I had to use self-defense. I'm not counting on it this time.

Sasha glares at us from just outside the hatch, backed up by two helmeted, uniformed crew holding tranq guns. She looks like someone has poured a vat of cold soup over her head. In spite of my terror, my lips twitch.

"I am through chasing you," she says. "Shoot them."

"I DON'T DO TAP," I mumble to the tentacled bovine standing next to me. "The shoes are just so noisy."

"That's why I go for the soft shoe." A purple tentacle holds out a black loafer with a suede sole. "Sprinkle a little sand, and shuh-sh-shuh away." The animal does a shuffle-ball-change step, dancing across the room on its hind legs, disappearing into a thick bank of fog.

I squint, and the fog resolves into a bank of cargo lights glaring down into the hold. I'm lying on my side, arms pinned behind my back, beside a pile of crates. A float panel moves along an aisle a few meters away, with the sound of grinding sandstone. Or bovine soft shoe. I turn my head slowly, to keep the tranq hangover at bay for as long as possible.

O'Neill lies on the floor next to me. At my movement, he turns his head and smiles. My heart flutters and my stomach warms, even lying on a cold cargo hold floor, trussed up like a roast beef. Do they truss roast beef? Julian would know.

I pull my wandering mind back to the problem at hand. "What's going on?"

O'Neill jerks his chin toward me. "DiFilippi got us. She and her cronies want to put us on ice. Literally. They're behind you. No, don't look yet." He keeps his voice low. "They're arguing over whether they can shove us both into one box. Apparently, they're almost out of storage lockers."

"Much as I enjoy spending time with you, I'd prefer not to do it in a freezer box." My voice cracks, and a couple tears leak out of my eyes. I blink them away. "I'm okay," I say in response to O'Neill's unasked question. "How do we get out of here? And who is she working with?"

O'Neill wrinkles his nose. "Countryman and DiFilippi are the ones arguing. There are a couple guys I don't recognize—I think they're the muscle. Ollie came in a few minutes before you woke up. He's staying well away from the other two, and has a weapon drawn. I think they might have tried to take him out that night in Ops. If you can roll over, you'll be able to see better. Besides, I want to get a look at how they tied us up. Move slowly, so they don't notice we're awake."

I give him a wan smile and slowly roll toward him onto my stomach. My feet seem to be connected to my hands, and they're bent up behind me. I can't really feel them—they've gone numb. With a heave of hips and shoulders, I get over onto my other side. O'Neill mutters a curse. I must have rolled a bit closer than I expected and probably whacked him with my feet.

"Bastards. Hang on," he whispers. "Keep an eye on those two and let me know if they come over this way."

Across a wide-open space, Countryman and DiFilippi stand next to the freezer door. She still looks like she's been run through an auto-bot-cleaner and then dipped in grease. Next to her, he's polished and crisp. They're arguing fiercely, but I can't hear any of it above the droning noise that marks the passing of another float panel. They must be pre-positioning their "cargo" for unloading.

Behind my back, I can feel O'Neill's breath on my wrists. My fingers are numb, but the warm air sends tingles up my arms. His lips send another shiver through my body. "I might actually be able to untie this. They used twine!" He sounds disgusted. "I guess I should be glad they didn't have any zip ties, but seriously, when we get home, I'm recommending a complete training program for cruise line security."

I swallow a slightly hysterical laugh and keep my eyes on the incompetent duo. A movement draws my attention to the other side of the room. Ollie sits in his float chair, a huge blaster held loosely in his hands. Behind him, another minion lurks. When Ollie turns his head toward me, I shut my eyes and press my hands against O'Neill's face to stop him moving.

With my eyes closed, all I can hear is the droning of the float panels. I open my eyes to slits and look at Ollie. He's focused on Countryman and DiFilippi, again. I wiggle my fingers, or at least try to, and Ty brushes his cheek against my arm before getting back to the twine.

"Hey, whatever you're going to do, we need to do it soon!" Ollie yells across the room. The two security agents turn to glare at him. "I have to go back on duty in a few hours. I need to cover for that one, so no one notices we've lost *another* crew member." He gestures toward us with his giant gun, shaking his head in disgust.

The bonds holding my feet release, and my knees jerk in response. I hold as still as possible, slowly unfolding my body while the others are watching each other.

"If you hadn't made such a stink about Les, Moore would never have gotten involved," Sasha yells back. "You *carpet sprinklered* this one all by yourself, Ollie!"

"You put my boss into the freezer!" Ollie yells back. Another float panel nearly drowns out his voice. "And I would have been next if *he* hadn't been called away from Ops at the last second. Is that kind of back-stabbing supposed to make me feel all secure and team-playerish?"

"Can we just figure this out and get out of here?" Countryman's voice is strained. "This place gives me the creeps."

Sasha shakes her head. "You are such a wimp. Why don't you both go back upstairs to your comfy jobs and leave me to clean up your mess. Like always." She turns back toward the long, low box beside her. The last freezer box.

Another float panel passes above us, but this one sounds different. Quiet, more of a hum than a grinding sound. I look up and see nothing. I keep staring, trying to figure out where the sound is coming from.

Then movement catches my eye. Above the three-high stack of crates behind O'Neill, there's a flicker of white.

A drone.

Like the ones used in the StarDeck to film the dance competitions.

CHAPTER THIRTY

"TY!" I spit the word out softly between gritted teeth. "Look up there. On top of the crates."

He stops chewing at my bonds and looks up. At least I assume that's what he's doing—I can't really see him.

"What did you see?"

"I'm not sure. It might have been a figment of my imagination. Just watch." I roll a little, trying to make my position less uncomfortable, but it doesn't help. But if I twist my neck, hard, I can catch a glimpse of Ty's face, down near my butt, and presumably my numb hands.

Across the room, Countryman says something to DiFilippi, and she grates back. But we aren't paying any attention, because at that moment, a spiky tuft of silver hair pokes over the edge of the top crate. Followed by two sparkling blue eyes. The left one winks, and the head withdraws.

"Joan," I whisper.

O'Neill chuckles. "We should have known she'd show up."

"Is that a drone?" I squint up at the ceiling, but whatever I saw has moved above the suspended lights, hovering in the shadows.

"Did you hear that?" O'Neill asks. "Joan had better be quiet. If those float pads stop moving, they'll hear her."

I gaze up at the top of the crates. Something is moving up there, but it's too small to be a person. I squint. Is that a string? With something tied to the end? As I watch in fascination, the tiny item drops lower and lower until it settles on O'Neill's hair. He muffles a yelp.

"Joan just lowered down a holo-ring." I shake my head in admiration. "Can you get it?"

"I've almost got you untied, I think." He jiggles his head, and the ring slides forward, the string arresting its fall. It slips across his face and down near my hands. "Can you get that?"

"There's no feeling in my hands," I say, panic sprinkled into my voice, despite Joan's near miraculous appearance. "How am I going to get it on? And what am I going to do anyway, if I can't see or feel it?"

"Trust Joan—I'm sure she has a plan. Just hold still a minute."

O'Neill's face rubs against my forearms, sending those warm shivers up to fight with the panic. I take a few deep breaths and try to focus on the argument still raging across the room. But all I can think about is what will happen to us if they put us in one of those freezer boxes. Where are they sending all those people? Slavery still exists in hidden pockets of the galaxy. I have no desire to see it firsthand.

"There. I got it on your finger. You really didn't feel any of that? It was kind of turning me on," he jokes.

I hear a faint click, and a voice sounds through my audio implant. "Pairing with new device. Continue?"

"Flick the ring again," I whisper. "It's asking to pair."

Another faint click. I think it's O'Neill's teeth against the ring.

"Pairing terminated."

"Zark! You hit the wrong icon! Do it again."

It takes three tries before we finally get the zarking thing paired.

"Connecting to holo-ring. Call inbound."

"You did it!" I hiss.

"Triana, this is Joan, can you hear me?"

"Joan!" I go limp with relief. "How'd you— never mind. What's your plan?"

"We're going to get some evidence, Triana." Joan sounds like the Marine she is—crisp and efficient. "I need you to get DiFilippi's attention."

I shrug, or at least try to. It's surprisingly hard to do when you're tied up on your side. "That should be easy enough." I take in a deep breath and raise my voice. "Hey, you parasites! Untie me over here!"

The arguing stops, and they all turn to look. DiFilippi raises her weapon.

"Don't let her tranq you again, though," Joan says in my ear.

"How am I supposed to do that?" I mutter.

"Just get her talking. Ask her where she's taking you." O'Neill whispers. "I think I know what Joan is up to."

I'm glad someone does. "Untie me!" I holler again. "I can't feel my arms. And it's cold down here."

DiFilippi stalks across the room. As she approaches, a wave of garlic and vinegar washes over me. I start coughing. That was some strong soup Julian dumped. My nose wrinkles and my eyes water.

She notices. "Lovely aroma isn't it?" she grits out. "Thanks for that. If I weren't in a hurry to get off this tub, I'd see to it your friends in the kitchen got what they deserve." She pokes me in the stomach with the nose of the weapon. "At least I can be sure you will."

"Keep her talking," Joan says. "Ask questions."

"Wha-what do you mean?" I stutter.

I can almost *hear* Joan shaking her head sadly.

I try again. "Where are you taking us?"

"You'll find that out soon enough," DiFilippi says. "If you think I'm going to stand here and tell you all my plans like some *Ancient TēVē* villain, you need to get your head examined." She raises the weapon. "Too bad you won't have an opportunity for that where you're going."

"Wait! You like *Ancient TēVē*?"

"No, I think it's ridiculous. But I heard you and O'Neill talk about it. It's a shame you had to do this the hard way. And I'm disappointed I had to wrap O'Neill up in all this. He's a real *pleasure* to work with." She tries to give her voice a sexy growl, but it just doesn't work for her.

"Please. He could tell you were dirty from the minute you showed up," I say, wondering why Ty hasn't chimed in here. He must see some value in pretending to be out. "There was no way this would ever have worked out for you and him to 'work' together."

"Ask her about the freezer," Joan whispers.

"Who are all those people you got frozen over there?" I ask. "And where are you taking them?"

DiFilippi shakes her head. "I'm not going to tell you anything. You're wasting my time, and I have product to move." She points the weapon at me, and the last thing I see is her greasy, grinning face.

"TRIANA! Triana! Nope, she's still out," Joan's voice says in my ear.

"I'm here," I mutter. "And I'm done talking to that *sink*." Even at this low volume, the OS catches my swearing. "*Packing box coffee table dish!*"

"That's fine. I'm sorry you got tranq'd. Can you open your eyes?"

I peel my eyelids apart. I'm lying on the floor, but when I squirm around, O'Neill is gone. "I don't know where Ty is!" My voice ratchets up a few octaves.

"Sh! It's okay. Don't let them know you're awake. He's still by the crates. I hit you with a stim before they dragged you across the room. You're by the freezer. Now listen, we need them to load you in the box and put you in the freezer before we can move in."

"What!?" I clamp a hand over my mouth. "Hey, my hands are free!"

"Yeah, O'Neill got through the twine before DiFilippi tranq'd you again. They figured you broke the string. But they decided it wouldn't matter if you were loose, because they plan to get you in the freezer before you wake up." Joan laughs. "You should have heard Sasha yell at Countryman for his incompetence."

"I'm sure this is entertaining for you," I grind out the words between clenched teeth. "But I have no desire to be a human popsicle. And where is O'Neill?!"

"He's fine. They tranq'd him again, too. He hasn't moved. I hit him with another stim, so he's ready to act as soon as you're in the box."

"Why do you keep wanting me to go in the box?" I shudder, just thinking about it.

"I want to make sure we have enough evidence to put them away," she replies. "We've got them on kidnapping you and O'Neill, but I need hard evidence to tie them to the people in the freezer and the ones you found on SK2."

I don't answer.

"Triana?"

"What do you mean about evidence to put them away?" I ask.

"Don't you want them to go to prison?" She sounds puzzled.

"Well, of course, but I want to survive more than I want to put them away." I don't see anyone around, so I sit up. Carefully. "You aren't really a retired Marine dance instructor, are you?"

She laughs again. "I never taught dance in the Marines, if that's what you mean. But I really am a retired Marine, and I really am a dance instructor. I have a friend in the agency who was investigating strange disappearances on cruise ships. So, when she heard I was working this one, she asked me to look into things. When DiFilippi grabbed you, I commandeered the dance show's drones to get concrete evidence."

"Don't you have to warn them they're being filmed, if you want the evidence to be admissible in court?" I rub my hands together, trying to warm them up.

"It's in their contract," she says, smugly.

I laugh. I laugh so hard tears roll down my cheeks. It probably sounds a bit hysterical, but I manage to keep a lid on the volume, since I know there are killers nearby. Well, not killers. Slavers? Freezers?

I take a few deep breaths and get myself under control. "What's the plan? What do you want me to do?"

"You are awesome, Triana," Joan says, warmly. "Here's the plan. I have the drones filming. It's being broadcast live, but I'm sure they're cutting in dance sequences from upstairs right now, since a woman talking to herself in a cargo hold doesn't sell cruise tickets."

A male voice cuts in. "That's affirmative, Joan. As soon as something interesting happens, we'll cut back to you, Triana. See if you can get them talking again."

I give an ironic thumbs up in the general direction of the ceiling.

"Ty is awake. I got close enough to talk to him, and I managed to get a knife to him. We didn't have another holo-ring, so he isn't patched into the conversation, but he knows the plan and he's ready to leap in and rescue you at a moment's notice. DiFilippi and Countryman were rearranging the rest of the cargo—or at least supervising—but they're all on their way back to you right now. Lie back down and close your eyes. We want them to think you're still out."

"How am I supposed to get them talking if I'm pretending to be unconscious," I grumble.

No one answers, so I lay down and close my eyes.

Footsteps clump closer, and the whine of a float panel gets louder. A thump and a whoosh of air tells me when the thing lands. Rough hands roll me over a couple times, onto the floater. I try to remain limp.

"This one ain't a lightweight, is she?" says a voice I don't recognize.

What the—? Who the zark is this creep who thinks he can talk about my weight while I'm out cold?!

"Easy, Triana," Joan whispers. "Don't give away the game!"

I grit my teeth and try to relax the rest of my body. It doesn't work very well, but by this time they've got me onto the float panel. It presses up against my body, lifting me a short distance. Suddenly, the panel tilts, and I tumble into the box.

"Hey! What the *pencil*!?" I sit up, rubbing my elbow. "Don't damage the goods, you *keyboard!*"

"We're live, with a two second delay!" The male voice says jubilantly. "Get them talking, Triana!"

The two goons operating the float panel point their weapons at me.

I hold up my hands. "No. Just no. I've been tranq'd enough for a lifetime. Besides, you're on a live broadcast, beaming into millions of homes. Wave to the cameras, boys." I wiggle my fingers toward the ceiling.

"Way to be subtle, Triana," Joan says with a sigh.

"No, this is great!" the broadcast dude says. "Get 'em riled up!"

"Maybe it's great for you—I'm trying to gather evidence!" Joan says.

Meanwhile, the two goons are staring around the room, looking for cams. "You're supposed to be out cold," the goon wearing a green shirt says.

The guy in the stripes takes a step back and looks around again. "What do you mean we're on cam? I don't want my mom to see me like this!"

I bite my lips. "I'm sure your mom has better things to do. But just in case she doesn't, maybe you should help me out. Then she can brag about her son the hero."

Stripes nods, but Green swacks him in the shoulder. "She's bluffing about this whole thing. There aren't any cams. She's just trying to get us to help her." He narrows his eyes at me. "I've got your number. Now lay down so I can close the lid."

"Uh, no, not going to happen. I'm not letting you freeze me. And I'm telling the truth about the cams. Just ask DiFilippi." I smile at Sasha as she walks into view.

Sasha growls. The two guys look at her, then at me, then at each other.

"What's it going to be, boys?" I ask. "Are you going to do Sasha DiFilippi's dirty work, throwing an innocent woman into the freezer and selling her into a life of slavery?" I point to my chest in case they aren't bright enough to know who I'm talking about. "Or are you going to come to the light side and save me? Make your mother proud, Stripes."

"Are you talking to me?" The goon in the stripes points at his own chest. "I'm Riley Timberman el Faheer. Who's this Stripes guy?"

Green smacks him in the arm and points to the stripes on his shirt. "She *is* talking to you, you idiot."

"Both of you shut up," DiFilippi barks. "Stick her with the drugs, shove her down into the box, and go get the guy. I want these two frozen now! I already have a buyer lined up for both of them."

"Got her!" Joan yells in triumph.

"Cut to commercial!" the broadcast dude says at the same time.

"I don't think so." O'Neill steps out from behind a crate, Ollie's blaster pointed at DiFilippi.

"Wait, don't cut to commercial!" the voice shrieks.

"Who untied him?!" DiFilippi howls. "Shoot him! Shoot him!"

Stripes and Green look at each other, then at DiFilippi.

"I said shoot him!" DiFilippi reaches for her holstered weapon.

Stripes tackles her, slamming her into the wall. "I want my mom to be proud."

CHAPTER THIRTY-ONE

THE REST of the night is exhausting but completely uneventful. O'Neill and Joan throw DiFilippi and Countryman into their own cell. Ollie is confined in one of the empty staterooms, and I take great pride in writing a code loop that makes his float chair inoperable outside that room. Kindra, Random and I decide to split the remaining shifts three ways. With the two of them on different schedules, maybe they won't be as likely to wander away. Plus, the threat of having their actions scrutinized by headquarters should keep them on the straight and narrow.

Once confronted with the overwhelming evidence, Ollie was ready to talk. O'Neill and Joan took turns questioning him, and he came clean in record time.

"According to Ollie, Timmons wasn't involved at all. Les was in it up to her eyeballs. Sasha put Les on ice because she, Les, was getting too close to Timmons. Sasha was afraid she'd tell him what was going on." O'Neill says. "Of course, we'll question him, and Les, when we get to port."

It's late the next afternoon. We've all slept a solid seven hours, and we're having a meal in the Maia suite. Technically, I've been on duty since noon, but, taking a page from Random and Kindra's playbook, I've forwarded only the emergency calls to my holo-ring. So far, my autoresponder seems to be doing its job:

You've reached Ops. If this is a real emergency, activate the red icon. If it isn't, file a ticket or fix the problem yourself. We will penalize any false emergency calls.

I think I've gained a little bit of a reputation on this ship.

"Did she think Timmons would cut her out of the scheme?" I pick up a spoon and pull a dish of ice cream toward me.

"Actually, we think she was afraid he'd turn her in. Timmons may be fast and loose in his social life, but he's pretty by-the-book everywhere else."

"Did they figure out how to revive the people in the freezer?" I pour some chocolate sauce on the ice cream.

"No, but we think the information might be hidden in DiFilippi's files. She was definitely running the show on this ship." Joan pours some tea into a heavy mug and adds a single spoonful of sugar.

"Vanti has a team ready to take the ship apart when we dock," O'Neill says. "The passengers are going to be transferred to a new cruiser at Crippen-Hauck—after they've been individually cleared, of course."

Vanti always manages to swoop in and save the day.

"Speaking of Vanti," I say casually, "what was she doing on S'Ride?"

O'Neill gives me a look. "She's investigating rumors of a slavery ring."

"Really?"

"Well, she is now." He smiles, but it fades quickly. "Actually, she's still chasing the funding the TLO received. The trail led to S'Ride. Coincidence? Maybe. Or maybe this little human trafficking scheme is part of Bobby Putin's twisted empire."

When I was on Kaku for training a few months ago, we cracked a terrorist group called the TLO and discovered it was funded by serial killer—and my former neighbor—Bobby Putin. "Wouldn't that be a huge coincidence? Kind of hard to believe it's all one big conspiracy."

"We know the Putins have several massive holdings on S'Ride." O'Neill ticks the points off on his fingers. "We know Bobby was funding his cleanup crew from sources other than the family wealth. And Vanti says she's uncovered more evidence. She'll tell me more when we meet in person."

We eat in silence for a few minutes. I'm not sure how I feel about spending time with Vanti. Maybe I'll be too busy with the Family Meeting. On second thought, I'd rather hang out with Vanti.

"What about the interns?" I lick my spoon and add some whipped cream and sprinkles to the bowl. "Steve? TC? Sandrine? And what about Ser Skeevy? He was down in the hold."

"The kids were clean. TC got sucked in to get to you," Joan says. I wince but Joan shakes her head. "Not your fault. Sandrine was trying to find a sugar daddy, but there's nothing illegal about that. Ser Skeevy *is* skeevy, but he was clean, too. He was down in the cargo hold with Timmons checking on the antiques he purchased on Grissom." She laughs. "And Steve was just Steve."

"Poor Steve," O'Neill says. "Assumed guilty by association. He really was trying to help us."

"He was trying to help a macho dude cheat on his girlfriend," I say. "I don't feel sorry for him at all. Besides, he beat Ambar out for the junior purser stint."

"Yeah, this was not Ambar's week." O'Neill shakes his head.

"Speaking of Ambar," Joan stands up, "we need to meet her in the Star-Deck in one hour. Are you ready for the big show?"

"I can't believe you're going through with the performance!" I wipe my mouth with a napkin. "Didn't the dance show get enough live coverage from us last night?

"But we didn't dance, so I still owe them. At least, that's what my contract says." O'Neill grins.

THE STARDECK IS PACKED. The show is being streamed to every cabin on the ship as well as the millions of homes down on Sally Ride, with an option to syndicate to the rest of the Galaxy.

Omar, the voice in my ear last night, is here in person, and he is ecstatic. "That bust really broke viewership records! Everyone is going to be watching, tonight."

"I hope they aren't disappointed," I say. "We don't expect any smugglers or slavers to show up today."

"That's okay, we get enough drama from the dancers." Omar grins and winks.

I take my seat at one of the front tables as the lights dim. Lu-wei Marchiano, the deep voiced announcer, grabs the mic and warms up the crowd. He tells a few lame jokes, which garner way more laughs than I think they should. He introduces the three judges—all of them formerly famous dancers and actors who have resorted to exchanging a stint on the show for free luxury transportation.

Then the competition starts. Lu-wei introduces the passenger first, then their crew member partner, and the dance instructor who trained them. This show must have much more of a following than I thought, because the crowd goes wild over the instructors. They're celebrities in their own rights.

Each team performs, then is interviewed while the judges deliberate. I smile and applaud at all the right places, waiting for Ty and Ambar to appear. When they do, I'm not disappointed.

Ty looks fantastic in a dark fitted suit with a bright white shirt. It's tastefully buttoned and finished off with an untied bow tie—so much better than the silver and black pirate costume open to the navel that the last dancer sported. Ambar is stunning in a tight black sparkling dress with a slit to the mid-thigh and a sweetheart neckline. The lack of bare flesh is a marked contrast from the previous teams.

After the polite applause for the couple, Joan struts onto the stage. She wears a pair of full pants that almost look like a ball gown, with a sleeveless, fitted top that shows off her slender figure and well-toned arms. A jaunty hat—apparently her trademark—perches amid her spiky silver hair. With a brilliant smile, she spins three times and takes a bow. The crowd erupts.

"I see this lovely woman needs no introduction! Three-time Galactic Pro Champion and *Dancing Through the Stars* Master Instructor, 'No Bones Joan' Lesley!" The applause gets even louder.

Across the room, Ser Skeevy and Sandrine sit together at a table. Sandrine is talking earnestly, but Skeevy's eyes are glued to Joan. Looks like Sandrine's days as a sugar baby are numbered.

The dance goes pretty well. Ty performs flawlessly. Ambar confines her mistakes to a few missteps and a tiny pause before the Alturan Timing. When they finish, she's grinning from ear to ear, and Ty looks pleased. He glances at me and winks.

I don't pay any attention to the interviews until I hear Ambar say my name. "...because she supported me even when I wasn't very nice to her. Thanks, Triana." She smiles, and it's completely open and friendly.

Wow.

She must really be feeling good.

AFTER THE WINNERS ARE ANNOUNCED—AMBAR and Ty came in second behind the Grendel and a scrawny little guy from Propulsion—O'Neill comes over to my table. He sits down and orders a glass of Zendarian Prosecco.

"What did you think?" He takes a sip and pretends he doesn't care how I answer.

I look at his perfect hair, his handsome face, his sexy, retro costume. "I think you are the shiniest man I have ever met."

We clink glasses. "And you are the most amazing woman I have ever met. Even if you are a space janitor."

IF YOU ENJOYED THIS STORY, you can read the next installment of Triana's adventures in Sweeping S'Ride.

ACKNOWLEDGMENTS

At the risk of being redundant, thanks to my family: my husband, David, who climbed up on the roof to the shovel the snow while I finished the last chapter, and my kids who stayed off the icy roads so I didn't have to worry about them. Thanks to Pippin the Wonder Westie who keeps me company, and only interrupts when it's time to go for a walk, or chase some snowballs, or bark at the UPS guy.

A big thanks to my sister, writer A.M. Scott, who reads all my crappy first drafts, and helps me figure out where the heck I went wrong. Thanks to my beta reader, Winnie St John, for taking the time to find my errors.

I'd like to give a shout-out to dance instructor Chris "No Bones" Jones, who taught me swing back in the last millennium, and who inspired me to have a Marine dance instructor. And to my friend Becky Lukens, who bears a striking resemblance to Joan.

Thanks to the great team at IPH Media: my editor Graham Erly, and my tech support guy Dave Arthur. Thanks to Les at GermanCreative for the cover. And a big shout-out to all the indie writers on 20BooksTo50K©, Story Origin, the Mystery Authors and the Indie Cover Project Facebook pages. Your advice and companionship are amazing.

And as always, thanks to the Big Dude for making all things possible.

ALSO BY JULIA HUNI

Colonial Explorer Corps Series:

The Earth Concurrence

The Grissom Contention

The Saha Declination

Colonial Explorer Corps (books 1-3)

Recycled World Series:

Recycled World

Reduced World

Space Janitor Series:

The Vacuum of Space

The Dust of Kaku

The Trouble with Tinsel

Orbital Operations

Glitter in the Stars

Sweeping S'Ride

Triana Moore, Space Janitor (the complete series)

Tales of a Former Space Janitor

The Rings of Grissom

Planetary Spin Cycle

Waxing the Moon of Lewei

Krimson Empire (with Craig Martelle):

Krimson Run

Krimson Spark

Krimson Surge

Krimson Flare

Krimson Empire (the complete series)

If you enjoy this story, sign up for my newsletter, at juliahuni.com and you'll get free prequels and short stories, plus get notifications when the next book is ready.

Milton Keynes UK
Ingram Content Group UK Ltd.
UKHW030730291024
2435UKWH00025B/132